MW01110058

StepFamilies

Step-

New Patterns

Families

in Harmony

Linda Craven

JULIAN MESSNER
New ·York

Copyright © 1982 by Linda Craven

*All rights reserved including the right of
reproduction in whole or in part in any form.
Published by Julian Messner
a Division of Simon & Schuster, Inc.
Simon & Schuster Building,
1230 Avenue of the Americas,
New York, New York 10020.
JULIAN MESSNER and colophon are trademarks of
Simon & Schuster, Inc.*

Manufactured in the United States of America

*First Paperback Printing, 1983
Design by Irving Perkins Associates*

10 9 8 7 6 5 4

Library of Congress Cataloging in Publication Data

*Craven, Linda.
Stepfamilies, new patterns of harmony.*

*Includes index.
Summary: Proposes positive approaches to conflicts such as lack of family unity, discipline
difficulties, sexual problems, loyalty issues, and
getting along with new brothers and sisters which
often become the points of contention in stepfamilies.*

*1. Stepchildren—Juvenile literature. 2. Step-
parents—Juvenile literature. 3. Family—Juvenile
literature. [1. Stepparents. 2. Family life]
I. Title.*

*HQ777.7.C73 1982   646.7'8   82-60652
ISBN 0-671-44080-2
ISBN 0-671-49486-4 Pbk.*

FOR MY STEPFAMILY:
CHRIS, SCHELLE, LAURI, DAVID, AND JERRY.
AND FOR ALL STEPFAMILIES EVERYWHERE.

Acknowledgments

I wish to express special appreciation to my writers group—Sam Pakan, Janda Miller, Jerry Hamby, Carroll Wilson and Jerry Craven—for their continued criticism and encouragement. Thanks to special friends and consultants: Ralph Desmarais, Joan Cave, Fred Rozendal and Tom Cannon Thanks to Emily and John Visher of the Stepfamily Association of America and to my editor, Jane Steltenpohl. My thanks also to Belle Ansley, without whose typing help I might never have completed the manuscript within the decade.

Most of all, thanks to my children and husband. Without their love, encouragement, suggestions and support, this book would have been neither conceived nor completed.

Contents

Is This Book For You?

If you are a stepchild or are about to become one, this book is for you. It's also for your parents. I have written it because my family and I have had to struggle through the special problems of living in step. And we know it isn't easy. I hope this book can make it easier for you.

In my work with stepfamilies, the same problems appear over and over again: loyalty conflicts, blaming, role and name confusion, stepparent/stepchild disagreements, lack of family unity, sexual issues, stepbrother/stepsister fights, and discipline difficulties. At the beginning of each chapter you will meet young people who have to deal with these and other stepfamily troubles. Perhaps their stories will help enlighten your situation by giving you and your parents new perspectives on these issues. Within each chapter you'll find out how some families learned to cope with each stepfamily problem. What worked for them might also work for you.

If you want, you can read just the chapters that seem important to you. Pass the book along to other family members so that you can all discuss the suggestions offered and how they might be applied in your case. Or you might have a family reading time when one member reads aloud to the others, stopping for discussion. Many stepfamily members say this kind of family meeting allows them to work through their toughest problems and come closer as a family.

Adjusting to stepfamily life isn't easy. If you are about to begin living in a stepfamily, you will find it more stressful than living in a traditional family—studies show this is true. If you already are a stepfamily member, then you know just how true.

But stepfamily living also has its rewards. For example, young people who grow up in stepfamilies often are more mature, more flexible and better able to cope with change than their peers from traditional families. You'll find out about many other advantages of living in step in these pages. And you'll learn how to use them in your life.

My stepfamily and I feel we've made it now as a family. We like living together (most of the time). But it was not always so. There've been many crises none of us were sure we'd make it through, especially in those early years together. I hope our experiences and those of the young people you'll meet in this book will help you through your own transition time.

Living in step isn't easy. But it can work. And it can be good.

Stepfamilies

Chapter One
StepFamily Myths

. SHANE .

I was fourteen and about to go into the ninth grade when my parents divorced. Sara, my little sister, went to live with Mom, but she came home for a visit at Thanksgiving. That's when Dad popped the news; for Christmas we were getting a new mother. Sara thought it was wonderful. She would be able to live with us. She and Dad laughed and cried and babbled about how great a person Rita is. I just asked to be excused, went to my room and tried to read.

The day Dad married Rita was the worst day of my life. I kept feeling homesick, only I couldn't go home and be all right, because I was at home. How many kids have to stand around smiling and nodding while one of their parents says "I do," and then kisses in public?

The house was full of people. Cake and punch were all over the place. And everybody was going around hugging everybody else, when most of them from the two different families hadn't even seen one another before. Rita's two kids were jumping up and down, playing games, dodging in and out of the crowd, while my sister, Sara, hung onto Rita nearly the whole time. She even asked, "Can I call you Mommy, now?"

after the ceremony. It made me sick. I could tell my Dad expected me to be jumping for joy, too, like everybody else. But I wasn't.

I was mad. Mad at Dad for being a traitor to my Mom. Mad at Mom for going off to law school and leaving us alone. Mad at the two brats, Rita's kids, who were going to come live in our house. Mad at Sara for liking them and their mother. But most of all, I was mad at Rita. In fact, as I watched her that day fluttering around in her ruffles and lace, feeding Dad cake out of her hand, I hated her. And because I believed it's not right to hate, I was mad at myself, too.

My grandparents took me home with them that night and I stayed a week while Dad and "my new mother," as Grandma called her, went on their honeymoon. "But I don't want a new mother," I told Grandma. "I already have one!" She went on and on about how people need a partner to help them through all the little ups and downs of life. When I reminded her Dad had a partner, my real mom, and asked why he couldn't just stay with her, Grandma just went right on with her harping as if I hadn't said a word.

It was Grandpa who made me feel a little better that week. We had several long talks late at night after Grandma was in bed. He was a lot more understanding than she was. He could listen. And hear. Maybe that's because he'd been in a similar spot himself. His father died when Grandpa was just a little boy, and his mother remarried after a few years. So Grandpa had a stepparent, too. But that was because one of his parents died. That seemed different somehow. I hated the word *stepmother*. And I hated the word *stepchild* even more.

Anyway, by the end of that week I'd decided I might as well accept the fact that my Dad had remarried and try to get along as best I could. Grandma had said how nice it was we'd be a "complete family" again, now, and how we could do lots of things together like work puzzles, go on picnics, play games together and stuff like that—like a family should. She said I'd feel a lot more secure now, with a new mother and sister and brother to love me, too. I wasn't so sure. But since I had been a little lonely ever since Sara left to live with Mom, I was hoping Grandma might be right.

Grandma was dead wrong. It didn't take long to figure that one out for sure. When I walked in the door, I saw right away that it wasn't my house anymore. It was hers. Rita had re-arranged the living room. And when I went to the bathroom, I found she'd switched my toothbrush and things from the big bathroom, the one I'd always used, to the little one. Rita was in the kitchen, and things in there were even more messed up. She was rearranging every cabinet in the place. "What's wrong with the way we put things away?" I asked her. "They weren't efficiently organized, that's what's wrong," she snapped.

Suddenly, I was afraid to look in my bedroom, and was even more horrified when I did. It had been rearranged, too. Only not just the furniture. Everything. My clothes and things had all been stuffed into half the drawers so Toby, her kid, could have the other half. Toys and piles of junk I'd never seen before were scattered all over the bed and floor along with some of my books and my stamp collection. Not only that, the picture of Mom I'd always kept on my desk was gone.

I blew up. I told Rita I didn't like her and her kids marching in and taking over like that. And she told me this was now their house too. Pretty soon we were yelling at each other. She called me a spoiled brat. I called her an ugly stepmother. Then I ran out of the house and walked the seven miles back to my Grandparents' house.

Storybooks often end with, "they lived happily ever after." But real-life stories seldom end that way, especially when the story is about a stepfamily. It's hard to learn to live with someone you don't know very well, especially if you would really rather not have to try. But even when everyone in a new stepfamily wants it to be a happy one, there are problems that no one expected.

Social scientists are only beginning to understand why. One reason stepfamilies have a great many problems is this: Almost all people have some beliefs about stepfamilies that just are not true. These beliefs come to us through our society—from stories we hear, from movies or television shows we see, or from things we hear people say. These beliefs that are not true are called myths. Any myths about stepfamilies and the people in them get in our way when we try to live together and to get along with each other. So the first thing we will do is to take a look at some of the myths about stepfamilies.

THE MYTH OF HAPPILY EVER AFTER

When people marry, it is usually because they believe they will be happier living together than they were not living together. Sometimes they are happier. Sometimes not.

Many stepfamily members, parents and children, are very happy about the remarriage and think everything in life will be better now. They believe that the new family will live happily ever after.

Then they're shocked and disappointed when things go wrong.

Shane's parents and his grandmother believed in the myth of happily ever after. They were unaware of Shane's feelings and unaware of the kinds of problems stepfamilies always face. Therefore, they were totally unprepared to deal with those problems and to give Shane the support and help he so badly needed.

It's not surprising that people believe in happily ever after.

Many of the stories we've heard or read end that way. Television programs and movies usually have happy endings, too. But real-life stories, like Shane's and yours and mine, are very different. In the first place, a real-family story has no distinct beginning or end like a storybook or TV program does. For example, would you say your own story began with the remarriage? The divorce? Your birth? Your parents' first wedding? Your grandparents' wedding? And when will your story end? When you start to college or go to work? When you get married? When your children are grown? When you die? When your children die?

In real situations, family lives are continuous, stretching back into the past and forward into the future, generation after generation. New family members appear from time to time as a result of births and marriages, while other family members move out of the picture as a result of growing up or choosing to live elsewhere, or because of death. But there are no distinct beginnings or endings to our real stories. So, in real life, there can be no happy endings in the storybook sense at all.

Another problem with the happily-ever-after myth is that no person and no family ever truly lives happily ever after. Some people seem to have an easier time in life than others. And some families seem to live together more peacefully than others. But there is no one on earth who lives perfectly happily without his or her share of ups and downs, arguments, and other problems. No one. And there is no family, whether a first family or a stepfamily, that has no tension among family members, no conflicts, and no bad times.

Sometimes when we think back about our first families it seems as though life was much easier and we were much happier then. Life was beautiful. But people tend to remember only the good times. That's why, in every age, there is so much talk about the good old days. But there were bad times in the good old days, too. You can bet on it. And every family, step or no, must work through its daily ups and downs. There are no perfectly happy families. None.

The main reason the old happily-ever-after myth gets in the way of stepfamily relationships, however, is that it causes the family members to expect things to happen differently from the way they probably will happen. Shane's father, stepmother, and especially his grandmother expected everything to be wonderful after the remarriage. They had visions of picnics, games and other good times together as a family. They didn't know that all stepfamilies have more than their share of problems to work through.

If your family members believe that happy marriages are supposed to make people live happily ever after, you, your parents, and your brothers and sisters (if you have any) probably expect that your family should get along well without any really big upsets or big problems.

But that isn't likely. I don't know of a single stepfamily (and I know many) that hasn't had a great many problems to work out. You could say that it's only natural for there to be many problems in a stepfamily. Here's why.

In first families, there are only two people when the marriage begins—the parents. Usually these two people have a lot of time to get to know one another really well and to get used to living together before the first child comes along. When the wife does become pregnant, the couple then has several months to get used to the idea of having a child. And when the baby comes, the family gradually adjusts to having one more family member. With each additional child, the process is the same. Each family member is allowed to adjust gradually. There's plenty of time.

But a stepfamily beginning is very different. It's very sudden. The wife and husband have very little time alone to get to know one another really well and to get used to living with each other. And you, your brothers and sisters, stepparent, and stepbrothers and stepsisters are brought together all at once. There's no gradual adjustment time in a stepfamily.

Besides all that, you and your new family members already have your ways of doing things, like housework, or cooking, or having fun. And each of you probably believes, as most people do, that your way is the right way—because that's the way you and your family have always done it. If your ways and the ways of your new family members are not just alike, there's going to be trouble for sure.

For example, if your stepparent is a very neat person who likes everything in its place, and you are comfortable with your room being a little (or a lot) messy, then you and your stepparent might have disagreements over which way is right. If the two of you had been together since your birth, those things could have have been worked out gradually as you grew up.

And they will have to be worked out gradually now. If you and the other members of your stepfamily believe you should be perfectly happy together right away, then all of you will be disappointed. People don't learn to live together happily overnight. It takes time. Lots and lots of time.

Another of the reasons stepfamily members often expect to live happily ever after is that they have watched "The Brady Bunch," or "Eight Is Enough," or other TV programs or movies about stepfamilies. These shows give the impression that the families are typical stepfamilies and that their only real problems are simple issues such as whose socks are whose, or who will do the dishes tonight. Again, these stories are not like real-life stories at all. The people you see in those programs are actors. They are not even members of the same family except during the show. If we could actually put all the people you see on one of those programs together in a house and have them try to live as a family for just one week, believe me, they would have some real problems! They would fight with one another and have arguments and scream and cry and pout just like real people do. Just like members of real families do. Especially stepfamilies.

But many stepfamilies become very close and the members all like one another. They learn to respect and sometimes even to love one another. They have all the normal ups and downs, but they have no more problems than any other family. In the truest sense, they are happy people in a happy family.

But it doesn't happen overnight. The average adjustment time for most stepfamilies is about five years. That's right! It takes most stepfamilies about five years, sometimes more, sometimes less, to work out their major conflicts so that they really like living together (most of the time).

The Myth of the Ugly Stepmother

You've probably heard the stories of Snow White and of Hansel and Gretel. And everyone knows the story of Cinderella, the kind, sweet stepchild who was treated cruelly by a wicked stepmother and ugly stepsisters. Cinderella was worked too hard and loved too little. Everyone who's ever heard her story is glad that it's Cinderella, and not her stepsisters, who gets the prince.

It's a lovely old story. There's just one problem with it. The story of Cinderella, like the stories of Snow White and of Hansel and Gretel, is not much like real life at all. There are no children (or adults) who are as pure and sweet as Cinderella appears, never saying or doing anything unkind, ever. And there are no adults (or children) who are as totally cruel and wicked as the despised stepmother and stepsisters.

Real-life people are both good and bad, kind and cruel, depending on the circumstances.

The story of Cinderella was written, as most stories are, for entertainment. It causes us to cheer for the heroine, to boo the villain, and then to rejoice when our favorite character wins over all the odds.

But events and people in real life don't function this way at all. It's very difficult to decide who the bad guys are in real-life stories, because each of us has both good and bad traits. Most stepparents want to be liked by their stepchildren (although some very few may not care). And few stepchildren are totally innocent and blameless in the conflicts that arise between stepparent and stepchild, or between stepsiblings (stepbrothers and stepsisters). There are always two sides to every story.

Did you ever wonder what the Cinderella story would have sounded like if told from the stepmother's or one of the stepsisters' point of view?

. *RITA* .

Rita had all kinds of fantasies about how wonderful their family life would be. She loved George and was sure, therefore, she'd love his children as well. She liked them already; Shane and Sara were polite, pleasant children. But she had the feeling their mother was a cold, insensitive person who put her needs before her children's needs. She knew Shane's and Sara's mother had never simply played with them, nor had she ever given them any individual attention. Rita was sure she could be the perfect mother to Shane and Sara, and she looked forward to fun evenings and weekends together with them and George and her own two kids.

What Rita hadn't expected was the sudden change that came over Shane after the wedding. He had seemed to like her before. They had all picnicked together, gone to movies together, played card games, and had great fun while she and George were dating. But the day of the wedding, Shane was suddenly surly and rude to her and her children. He ignored Rita when she spoke to him, except when she asked whether he liked the cookies she'd baked. "My Mom's are better," he'd snapped. Shane started row after noisy row with Tammy until Rita finally insisted they stay in separate rooms. And when Toby went into Shane's room just to look at the aquarium, Shane gave the little boy a bloody nose.

When it finally came time for the ceremony, George had to make Shane change into nice clothes and join the guests. Rita felt there were daggers of icy hate in his eyes when their glances met. And she'd never been more relieved than when Shane's grandparents took him home with them.

Later, Rita gave that day a lot of thought. She realized Shane must have been feeling upset about all the changes happening around him. And she determined to get Shane back on her side when he returned.

So Rita set about making plans. She and George and the children had talked earlier about the need for some rearranging in the house so that they could all live there together. But she felt Shane might resent having to help do all the work that would require. So she spent the day he was to return rearranging the household. She placed the bathroom items conveniently, so that each person's things were in the bathroom nearest his or her bedroom. She also moved Shane's clothes for him and put Toby's in place, leaving Tammy and Sara to manage theirs alone. Next, she switched the living room furniture around so that it would hold the two chairs she and George had purchased. They wanted every member of their new family to have a comfortable place to sit. Finally, Rita began rearranging the kitchen in a more orderly fashion, thinking of all the wonderful meals they would prepare and share together. As a final touch, Rita had asked George what

Shane's favorite foods were; she was preparing them for dinner.

But her hopes for a happy homecoming were soon dashed. "Who messed up the living room?" he demanded upon entering. When told that Rita had done the rearranging, "I should have known," he replied, stomped into the bathroom and slammed the door behind him. Shane rushed out again, however, and promptly accused Rita of taking over the bathroom that was his, without even asking. "And what's that smell?" he frowned. Shane piled one criticism upon another until, when he finally attacked Rita about the way she was rearranging the kitchen, she was feeling angry, too.

But it wasn't until Shane started yelling at Toby to get out of "his" bedroom that Rita lost her temper. She knew she shouldn't say the harsh things that came tumbling out, but she couldn't help herself. She had wanted, so badly, to be a good mother to Shane. And there she was, on their first day together, sounding like the ugly stepmother. Sure, Rita was mad. But most of all, she was hurt.

It's impossible to hear both Shane's and Rita's sides of their story without realizing they both made some mistakes, and they both were hurt as a result. Rita was too eager to become a mother to her new husband's children. She rushed in too quickly and failed to consult Shane about the rearrangement of their shared home.

Shane, on the other hand, hated the idea of having a stepmother and of being a stepchild. He watched for reasons to be angry, and found them without taking the trouble to understand just why Rita had done the things he didn't like. Shane expected Rita to be cruel and ugly. And he managed, through his unfair treatment of her, to get Rita to fulfill his expectations.

Neither Shane nor Rita was an evil, cruel person. Both were victims of stepfamily myths.

If they had only known, as you now know, that the myth of happily ever after and the myth of the ugly stepmother are untrue, perhaps they would have been better prepared for the problems of adjustment they had to face. Perhaps they would have been able to get along. They would still have had problems, of course. But Shane's and Rita's story could have been a happier one.

It's very difficult to put yourself in another person's shoes, to look at a situation from another's viewpoint. But real-life situations require that we do so at times. And when we do make the effort to understand the other's point of view, we find ourselves relaxing some, hurting less, simply from having a better understanding of the causes behind the actions that have been bothering us.

If you have a stepmother or stepfather, or soon will have, you can forget the old myth about the ugly stepparent. Your stepparent is who he or she is—a person with both good and bad qualities. And that person will not become wicked or ugly simply because of becoming a stepparent. Your own nature will not change, either, simply because you are a stepchild. Each of you will remain essentially who you are. And the relationship between you will be born out of that, if you allow it, and not out of the old myths at all.

THE MYTH OF INSTANT LOVE

Some people feel, as Shane's grandmother did, that simply because two people get married, their lives will be much happier than before. They also believe, as Rita did, that just because the two people love each other, they will automatically love each other's children and that the children will automatically love the new parent in return. They believe in the myth of instant love.

But love doesn't work that way. We can't love a person just because someone else wants us to or even because we believe we should. Love is like a wild bird. If you're very patient for a long time, it might come and eat the food you've offered. And it might not. But if you chase after the bird and try to force it to stay, it will almost certainly be frightened and fly away.

Like a wild bird, love can't be forced to come or to stay. If the members of a stepfamily believe they must love one another or that they should love one another, then they are likely to feel angry or guilty when they don't love or feel loved. But if you and the others in your stepfamily remember that love must be free, then you will expect no instant love and feel no guilt.

You do not have to love your stepparent. And your stepparent does not have to love you. But the two of you might decide to offer each other companionship and a fair chance for friendship. And if you both are very patient for a long time love, like a wild bird, may come to you.

Chapter Two
Too Much Change Too Fast

. TAMMY .

Everything had changed since her Daddy died. Everything.

Tammy was walking the six blocks from the junior high to the elementary school where she'd find her brother, Toby. From there they'd walk five more blocks to their new home where nobody waited for them.

They hadn't had to walk home in the old days, unless they wanted to. Mom was always there to pick them up. Then she'd stop by the grocery store where they'd all have a Coke while shopping for something for dinner. When they got home, Tammy and Toby watched their favorite TV programs until Dad came in. And after supper, they'd all go somewhere together, or watch TV together, or just joke around and have a great time together. They were a happy family. Then.

But all that had changed. Dad went on a business trip one weekend in the company plane and never came back. Since then, everything had changed.

"Hey, Toby! Cut that out!" Tammy spotted her nine-year-old brother rolling around in the dirt fighting with a boy about twice his size.

Toby was one of the things that had changed a lot since their father's death. Actually, he'd never been an angel, always into things, always in motion. But Toby had become even more rowdy and destructive, especially since those other people had come into their lives. Their mother had recently remarried. So Toby and Tammy had suddenly acquired a stepfather, a stepbrother, and a stepsister. Wham! Just like that.

Toby had since become a real troublemaker. Tammy grew angry with him sometimes herself, like the time she caught him scooting her favorite records across the floor, playing they were race cars.

But she felt sorry for him sometimes, too. Especially when she realized he usually caused more trouble for himself than for anyone else. Like now.

"Stop it!" she yelled, pulling the boys apart. "Why don't you pick on a kid your own size?"

"You're crazy," the older boy retorted. "I was just walking along, minding my own business, when this squirt lighted into me. All I did was defend myself."

Tammy recognized the boy now. His name was John, and she sat next to him in math class. He'd smiled and talked with her just that morning. Tammy had hoped they might be friends. "Come on, Toby," she said, wiping dirt and blood from his face. "Let's get you home."

"Hey, girl," John called after them. "You better teach your little brother some manners. He'll get himself killed like that someday."

Tammy ignored him. "Just look at you." She dragged Toby along. "What's Mom going to say when she sees your face? What's George going to say?" Tammy imagined the stern face of their stepfather peering down. "To your rooms," he would boom. "And no TV!" George was always sending them to their rooms. And he and his snooty kids were always making fun of TV. The "boob tube," they called it. In a strange town, in a new neighborhood where you didn't know anybody to hang around with, what was there to do but watch TV?

Toby picked up a rock and chucked it at a passing car.

"Toby!" Tammy grabbed his skinny arm. The rock fell short. "What's the matter with you lately?" she scolded. Then Tammy saw the tears in his eyes, put her arm around Toby, and they trudged on home together.

One of the most difficult problems stepchildren must face is change—too much change too fast.

All people experience major changes in their lives: We lose someone we love, we move to a new house and neighborhood or another town, new members are added to our families, or we change schools or jobs. When major changes like these occur one or two at a time, most of us can adjust—in time. But it often takes about a year, sometimes longer, for a person to adjust to a major change like a move or the loss of a family member.

All people, adults and children too, have much more difficulty, however, when too many major changes come along in too short a period of time. This is especially true when the change is not one we have chosen for ourselves but must simply live with, like it or not.

Like Tammy, most stepchildren go through many major changes within a short period of time. First, one of the biological parents may be lost, either through divorce or death. Next, the remaining parent must take on new roles and responsibilities. For example, the mother may have to go to work when the child has been accustomed to her being at home. Or the parent may take a different job which requires him to work different hours than before. In any case, whichever parent the child lives with must certainly take on more responsibilities both at home and at work than when there were two parents to share the chores and the daily workload. So a single parent inevitably has less time to spend with the child. In most cases, the child must also take on more responsibilities. These kinds of changes in routine generally bring about changes in the parent/child relationship.

Then remarriage occurs. And the child must adapt to the most traumatic change of all—living, day in and day out, with a stepparent and perhaps with stepbrothers and stepsisters too. On top of all those dramatic changes, new families frequently move, bringing about another whole set of changes —new friends, new school, new teachers, new neighborhood. No wonder the stepchild sometimes feels overwhelmed, angry or depressed. Anyone facing so many major changes in life would be upset. It's only human nature.

How to Deal with Change

There are many things you can do that will help you get through this time of transition in your life. There are two old beliefs that sometimes get in the way whenever we think about our problems: First, some people believe all their problems are caused by things outside themselves which they cannot control. It may have seemed to Tammy, for example, that all her troubles were caused by the move to a new town and by her new, and unwanted, stepfamily members. Second, there are other people who blame only themselves for all that happens. They believe all their problems are a direct result of their own personal faults and weaknesses. Neither belief is true.

Whenever we allow ourselves to believe all our problems are caused by someone or something else, we give up all our own personal power and our ability to make changes that might bring about solutions to the problems. Tammy may be overlooking some things she, personally, could do to make life easier.

At the same time, whenever we believe that we are bad, that our problems are entirely a result of our own faults, then we become depressed or unhappy and are thus not able to see possible solutions to our problems. Young Toby was not a bad child. He behaved badly by starting fights and throwing rocks. But even at those times, he was not a bad person; he was just a person behaving badly.

Each of us is both good and bad. Each of us can choose how to behave. And each of us has the power to bring about positive changes in our lives.

Stepfamily problems, like all problems, are never the result of one single thing or one single person's faults. Instead, our problems are complex. They are caused, in part, by too many changes happening too fast. They are caused by our parent's and stepparent's failures to recognize and understand our feelings. And they are also caused by our own failures to understand others and to behave in helpful ways. Happily, there are many ways to solve our stepfamily problems.

BE GOOD TO YOURSELF

The most important thing to remember, while there are so many changes occurring in your life, is to treat yourself well. The famous writer Mark Twain once said, "I can live for two months on a good compliment." All of us feel good when someone says or does something nice for us. But had you ever thought that you can also do nice things for yourself? You can be good to you. And you deserve it.

1. Make a time and place that is all your own.
   Every person alive has a need for privacy. Even the most friendly and outgoing of individuals needs a quiet spot

from time to time to do just what he or she likes to do. Or just to do nothing at all.

In a stepfamily there are often several people living under one roof. And a place of your own, or a time to just be alone is often hard to come by. You may share your bedroom with a sister or brother. And there may seem to be no other place in the house that you can call your own, especially if you spend only weekends or vacations in the home of your parent and stepparent. All of us need room. Even rats fight with one another when they're overcrowded and don't have enough personal space.

But there are some ways you can make, for yourself, the privacy you need. One way is simply, but nicely, to ask for it. Ask your parent to read this chapter. Then ask if you may have a special time and place all your own. If you share your bedroom, perhaps an hour of time could be set aside each day, say from four until five o'clock, for you to use the room all alone. A different hour could be your roommate's own special time. You might choose to use your hour to do homework, talk on the phone, write in your diary, listen to music, or just to be alone. The important thing is that it is your time and your space. And you can make the choice as to how to use it.

If you're unable to reach such an agreement with your other stepfamily members, then there are other ways to establish some privacy for yourself. Closets are sometimes large enough that you can make a little place for yourself inside. With a pillow propped against the wall, a closet floor is a great place to think, read, write or nap. Some houses and apartments have a little space under stairs that is not used, or a corner by the fireplace or entryway. Even a drawer that you know is your very own to put things in is helpful. Or you might get a box with a lock on it so you'll have a special place to keep things that are important to you. Ask your parent for assistance in establishing your right to privacy. Everybody needs space to be.

2. Ask for time alone with your parent.

I read a story once that made me very sad. It was a true story about some babies in a large nursery. The babies had no parents but were cared for by nurses who had only time enough to take care of the infants' physical needs. The babies were fed regularly. Their diapers were changed. They were bathed and kept warm and were given medicine when sick.

But none of the babies grew as fast as normal babies with parents do. And some of them died. They didn't die from disease. They didn't die from hunger or from exposure or abuse. The babies died simply because they weren't held and talked to and stroked and cuddled the way most babies are. They died from lack of love.

All creatures great and small need love. Even my son's salamanders, who fight at feeding time, crawl up into one big pile when they sleep. They like to be close to one another.

People have a need for closeness and love too. Doctors have discovered that even the most powerful of medicines cannot heal a person who does not feel loved. As the famous doctor Karl Menninger has said, "Love cures people—both the ones who give it and the ones who receive it." It is only natural that you should want your parents to show you that you are loved.

But some parents who remarry are so glad to have a special new relationship that they forget about some other important things, like their children's needs. Or they might just be so involved in new routines and responsibilities that they don't notice some of the other things going on around them. The time when they are learning to live in step is a time of great change for parents too.

It is important for you and your parent to maintain a good relationship during this time of change. It can be a source of strength for you both. That's not to say your parent should always take your side against your stepparent or stepsiblings. Quite the contrary. A parent's goal is to try to be as fair as possible at all times and to encourage the working out of problems. Sometimes the best thing a parent can do is to simply stay out of conflicts between child and stepparent or child and stepchild and allow them to work through their differences on their own. However, there are some things you can do that will help your parent recognize your needs and better meet them. A strong parent/child relationship can be a stablizing force. It can act as an anchor in the storm of change.

Ask your parent to read this section. And ask him or her to help you keep or make your relationship strong. You may find it difficult to ask directly for attention or love. If so, remember the words of Cecil Parker, "Behold the turtle who makes progress only when he sticks his neck out."

Tammy's little brother, Toby, needed more attention and love than he was receiving from his parents. It probably never occurred to him to ask for it directly. And no one ever suggested that he do so. Instead, Toby stayed busy getting himself in trouble. At least his parents paid attention to him when he behaved badly!

But Toby felt bad about himself. Even though he was getting the attention he craved, he felt neither loved nor loving. He was a miserable child. And all because he'd never learned to ask directly for the love he so badly needed.

Your parent may be as unaware as Toby's of your needs. He or she might not know that you would like some time and attention all your own—unless you say it right out loud.

You might begin by offering to help with some chore or task your parent must do, such as shopping, cooking or washing the dishes or the car. In this way, the two of you would be working side by side. You'd be together. Or you might request some special time to be set aside just for the two of you, such as Saturday morning, Sunday afternoon, or some weekday evening. Do something you both enjoy; take a walk, toss a ball or Frisbee, see a movie, play cards, or just visit. Many families use "tucking-in" time each night as a special time set aside for parent and child to visit and stay in contact with each other.

Touching is an important way of communicating feelings. If you and your family are comfortable with touching one another, do it often. If you are not used to touching, try it. Slip your hand inside your parent's or your sister's or your brother's. Squeeze Mom's arm as you pass by, put your hand on Dad's shoulder, brush your stepsister's hair. Be good to your family members and to yourself by giving and asking for the attention, time, and touching you need. Like salamanders, people need to stay in touch.

3. *Stay busy with things you like to do.*
Another way you can be good to yourself is to find something you enjoy doing, and do it. Perhaps you have a hobby or could develop one, such as collecting and learning about rocks or stamps or coins. Or you may like to build things, to draw or paint or play a musical instrument. Or maybe participating in sports is more your type of pastime. Then find others who like sports, too, and play often. In addition to being fun, physical exercise is also an excellent way to work off tension and relieve frustrations. The next time you're feeling angry, hurt or upset, go for a

bike ride or a swim, jog or take a long walk or play tennis or put on a record and dance. My high school speech and drama teacher made each of us memorize the phrase, "Motion breaks up tension." If we were nervous, she had us take a deep breath and move about until we felt better. Her method works as well in everyday life as it does on the stage.

Another way you can be good to you is to keep yourself looking nice. Personal grooming is important, not just so others will think we look nice, but because we feel better about ourselves if we know we are dressed in clean, neat clothes, our hair is combed, and our faces and bodies are clean. Getting enough rest and eating well are still other aspects of caring for yourself. And so is avoiding harmful substances such as tobacco, too much alcohol, or other drugs you don't need for medical reasons.

Your physical health and your emotional health are intertwined with each other as much as the individual links of a chain are. If just one link is weak, a chain cannot carry as heavy a load without breaking. If your body is weak, you cannot withstand the daily emotional stresses of stepfamily living.

4. Everyone needs a friend.

Most important of all, be good to yourself by talking with a friend about what happens at home. Problems that are kept secret grow heavier day by day, just as the trash can does if it isn't emptied regularly. But problems that are talked about tend to stay smaller, more manageable. Everyone needs someone who will listen.

But whom can you talk to? To whom can you tell the secrets of your heart? Who would be willing to listen and share your load? The answer is different for every person, but it's usually best to look for a friend who is older than you are, or at least your age.

Some parents are able to listen. Some are not. If one of your parents is able to lend an ear without blaming or becoming upset, then by all means talk to him or her. Or talk to a sister or brother if you are good friends.

But in most families, it's easier to find a sympathetic ear outside the household. An outsider is more likely to be objective and less likely to become upset as you talk. Grandparents, aunts, uncles, and other relatives sometimes make good listeners. A friendly neighbor is another possibility. The friend you walk to school with might be willing to listen to your problems, and you to hers or his.

How to Make a Good Friend

If you, like Tammy and Toby, are new in the neighborhood and don't have any relatives or close friends nearby, then how do you go about finding someone who is willing to listen? It takes time, of course. Friendships don't grow overnight. But it needn't take forever. And you can make it happen. Here's how.

Watch for the signs of potential friendship. Does the neighbor across the street smile and wave when you go by? Does the girl or boy up the block speak when you pass on the street or in the hall? Have you been offered a ride by someone on the block or been given directions about how to get somewhere in the neighborhood? Is one of your teachers pleasant and friendly? Watch for these kinds of signals. They mean potential friendships.

And send out signals of your own. Introduce yourself to others around you. Offer to help carry in the groceries for the woman or man next door. Suggest studying together to the kid down the street. Or take a Frisbee or ball out and see if you can find someone to toss with. Offer to run an errand for a teacher after school, or help a neighbor garden or shovel snow.

And while you're doing these things, strike up a conversation about the other person's interests. Almost everyone likes to talk about his or her work, school, or hobby. And soon you may find that person asking about your interests in return. A friendship may have begun.

But don't give up if the first person you approach does not respond. Some people just don't make friends easily. Just keep an eagle eye out for the signs of potential friendship. And continue sending out signals of your own. Soon you'll find the right person—one who can become a good friend and a good listener.

You must be a good listener, too. When your friend talks, try to listen beyond the words. Try to imagine how you would feel if you were in your friend's position. It usually isn't necessary to give advice or to try to solve his or her problems, though you can offer help if it seems appropriate. But most of the time, just having someone who'll listen is enough.

TRY WRITING IT ALL OFF

Many young people find that writing in a diary or journal is another good way to "talk out" their problems. The next time you're feeling down, try describing what you feel and why. You might begin with the sentence, "Today, I'm feeling [angry, sad, lonely, or whatever] because _____." And keep on writing until you've written down everything you can think of about what's happening in your life right now.

One of the nice things about writing is that you can say anything you like in any way you like without worrying about getting into trouble or hurting someone's feelings with your words. But when you do this, just be sure to put your writing away in a place that it won't be seen; even if that means tearing it up and flushing it down the toilet a few pieces at a time.

The very best way to share your load is to tell a good friend about it. But when your best friend is not around, or if you don't yet have one, then try pouring out your troubles on a page. Your troubles might grow lighter as you do. It's like rearranging your load of firewood. If the pile is all jumbled up and unorganized, then it's hard to get a good grip for carrying. But if you neatly stack the pile, it's much easier to handle. Writing is a way of organizing your thoughts and troubles. Once stacked up neatly in one sentence after another, your problems may seem more manageable.

Be good to yourself. Talk out your concerns right now, today, even if it's just to a pet, to a favorite stuffed animal or toy, or on a sheet of paper. Don't try to hide from your problems. Make a time and place all your own, ask for time with your parent, stay busy with things you like to do, and share your load with a friend. You are an individual with legitimate feelings and needs of your own. Be good to yourself; go after the things you need and want.

Chapter Three
Who's Who in the Stepfamily?

. MELANIE .

Melanie stood before the mirror struggling to fasten her coppery hair into a braid. Usually her fingers did it automatically. But tonight they acted more like webbed feet than fingers. "Quack, quack," she mocked herself in the mirror as the unruly hair sprang loose again.

Tonight was the night of the father-daughter banquet. But Melanie's father lived in another city. And Don, the man her mother had just married, was planning to escort Melanie. One part of her said she had to do this, another said she couldn't or wouldn't.

Okay, she thought, dividing her hair into three equal parts, one more time. Right over left, left over right . . . From the kitchen came the smell of chicken frying. Melanie's mom was happily putting together a box supper for them to share. Right, left, right . . . If she could just shut out that awful noise! Don was singing in the shower as obviously happy as Melanie was miserable.

Melanie would never have gone to the banquet if it had been left up to her. There was a chance she would win an award—Ms. Hartley said her sewing project was one of the best. But Melanie would have been content to receive the ribbon next week at school. Trouble was, Ms. Hartley had called Don personally. "You will be there?" she'd asked.

"We wouldn't miss it for a frog's foot." Don winked at Melanie. Her stomach did a flop flop (as if she'd swallowed the frog's foot), and it hadn't been the same since.

It wasn't that Melanie didn't like Don. He was nice enough (most of the time). But he was rather strange looking with his wild, woolly beard, and he had some weird ways. (He was also younger than her mother and that was embarrassing.) But that wasn't the real problem. It wasn't even his annoying habits, like opening his eyes wide and thrusting his face at Melanie when making a point. The real issue was that tonight's was a *father-daughter* banquet. And Don was not her father.

Ms. Hartley had said each girl would stand and introduce her father. How could Melanie do that? What would people think about their last names being different? And how would she refer to Don? Hello everybody, she could just hear herself announcing. This is my mother's young man. (That's how Melanie's grandmother introduced him. Oh brother!) She didn't want to call him her stepfather; she hated the term and suspected Don hated it, too. Well she sure wasn't going to call him dad. She had a dad and he wasn't Don. After thinking it through for the hundredth time, Melanie was back where she started—nowhere.

She tugged at her braid so hard that tears came to her eyes. That singing! Shut up, Don! she screamed inside her head. Right, left, right . . . Now the fastener . . . But Melanie's fingers slipped and the hair fell loose again.

"Your box supper's ready," her mother chirped from the kitchen. Melanie saw tears fall on the green dress her mother had bought for the banquet. Why hadn't she told them earlier that she just couldn't go? She knew why. They'd never understand. Maybe she could pretend illness now? She really did feel sick over the whole thing.

"Aren't you ready, honey?" her mother said and swung into the room. "Oh, having trouble with your hair? Why didn't you call? You know I can do it in a jiffy. Here. Now wipe away those tears. You and Don are going to be the most handsome pair ever. There, now. Just wait until you see your box supper; you'll love the way I wrapped it . . ."

Don appeared, reeking of cheap aftershave, in one of his weird, guru shirts. And they were swept out of the house on her mom's gush of words before Melanie managed to say a thing or to think of a way to keep from going.

And then they were there, seated with all the real fathers and daughters.

"Hi, Melanie," Tammy said, rushing over to sit beside them. "I thought you said you didn't want to come to . . ."

"Shhh!" Melanie warned.

"Hey, how come your eyes are red?" Tammy persisted.

"Don't ask now," Melanie's eyes darted toward Don.

"Oh," Tammy nodded. They both became very busy unloading their box suppers.

Throughout the meal Melanie was conscious of Don's poor table manners. He didn't put his napkin in his lap, he talked and laughed with the man across from them, even when his mouth was full, and bits of chicken fell here and there, on the table, on Melanie, on the floor. But worst of all was the globule of milk that dangled in his beard.

"Eat up, babe!" he said, noticing Melanie. She tried, but found the chicken dry and hard to swallow.

Then the thing she had been dreading most began—the introductions. There was one table ahead of Melanie's. She watched as one girl after another stood and proudly announced her father's name. But her own thoughts were louder than their words.

When her turn came, what would she say? This is my mother's new husband? No, that wouldn't do. Just plain Don Arnold? No.

The girl at the head of Melanie's table stood up. "I'm Jennifer Jarman," she said. "And this is my father, John West." Melanie had forgotten about Jennifer—she was a stepchild, too. But Jennifer had introduced Mr. West as her father! That didn't seem right, somehow; it seemed like a lie. But then Jennifer's stepfather had been in the family ever since Jennifer was just a little thing. Maybe that made it different.

Two more girls before Melanie. She felt ill and considered running for the bathroom but remained frozen in her chair.

One more.

"I'm Tammy Harper," the girl next to Melanie was saying.

My gosh, Tammy! Melanie said to herself. I'd forgotten all about Tammy's family.

"And this is my stepdad, George Doleman."

There it was, plain and simple. My stepdad. Everyone else applauded just as they had for all the other fathers and daughters. Tammy and George sat down.

It was Melanie's turn. She stood.

"I'm Melanie Morceaux," she croaked. "And this is my stepdad, Don Arnold." Don squeezed her arm gently as he rose to stand beside her.

There was applause. They sat down. Melanie felt a wave of heat rise from her neck up through her face. But the focus of the group had already shifted. Melanie had survived.

Melanie was miserable over a simple name. Most stepfamily members struggle with the problem of names—what to call and be called. It may seem a simple question. But it isn't. It's not only one of the first issues that arises after remarriage, it's also one of the most important. How can names be so important?

Our names identify us. They define who and what we are. And stepfamily members, like Melanie, struggle with what to call one another because they are not yet sure of their relationships. They're not clear as to who or what they are in relation to one another. They don't yet know who's who in the stepfamily.

The question of names is more than a question of what to call and be called. It's a question of identity. Who am I now? What role will I play? Is a stepparent a parent? Am I his or her child? How do I fit into the new family? Is a stepfamily a family? What will other people think? And how do we decide what to call one another?

The way you and your family decide the question of names is important, because in choosing what to call one another you begin to clarify your relationships. You begin to decide what kind of family you will be. And you begin to define the roles each of you will play in the family.

This chapter will help you understand the confusion of identity and names. It will explain why most people don't like the word *stepchild*. It will explore the different roles you, your stepparent, and other family members can choose. And it will help you decide which names to use. Finally, it will guide you toward an answer to the question, who's who in the stepfamily?

WHO WANTS TO BE A STEPCHILD?

Stepfamily. Stepmother, stepfather, stepchild. Stepgrandparent. Stepdaughter, stepson, stepbrother, stepsister. Stepuncle, stepcousin . . . The list goes on and on. But a lot of young people avoid using the words on that list. So do a lot of adults, especially if they are, themselves, steppersons. Do you also avoid the step terms? Do you know why?

One of the most common reasons for most of us is that when we speak of our stepfamily we are reminded that our original family no longer exists. Whether that is the result of divorce or death, the reminder is painful—it recalls something we've lost. The step terms also point out to us that we are different from our peers who still live in their original families. And most people, especially young people, don't like the feeling of being different.

But our reasons for disliking the step words go even deeper than pain from loss or discomfort from being different. They reach deep into the mystery of our beings and back to the very origin of our language.

Hundreds of years ago the Anglo-Saxon word *steōp* meant orphaned. It was used to refer to children whose parents had died or abandoned them. A *steōpbearn* was a child who had lost just one parent and whose remaining parent had remarried. Eventually, the term *steōpcild* came to be used for anyone or anything that was deprived or pitiful.

The step terms are occasionally still used in a derogatory way (but only by people who are insensitive). For example, one woman recently complained that her husband treated her "like a stepchild. I deserve better treatment," she exclaimed, as if a stepchild does not deserve to be treated well. I suggested that not all stepchildren are mistreated and that she might choose a different phrase to explain what she really meant. It is because the step terms have been used this way that some people feel uncomfortable using them to describe their family relationships. There are also numerous folktales about abused and neglected stepchildren. We have mentioned Cinderella, Snow White, Hansel and Gretel and others. Were there no stepchildren, in the old days, who had normal, happy lives? Surely there were. Then why haven't we heard their stories? The fact is, calm, happy lives make for dull storytelling, while stories of abuse and neglect are suspenseful and exciting. The old folktales are exaggerated stories of a few children's lives in the long ago and far away.

The trouble with those tales is that, as we hear them over and over again, we come to believe that every stepchild has a difficult life and is to be pitied.

Not so. It may be true that some Anglo-Saxon orphans were not treated well. But times have changed. Some experts feel that today's stepchild receives too many gifts and too much smothering from two sets of parents, four sets of grandparents, and numerous aunts, stepaunts, uncles, stepuncles, etc. Today's stepchildren have their problems (just as all kids do), but few of them are truly deprived or pitiful.

There is at least one other reason most people don't like the stepfamily terms. That reason has to do with current-day meanings of the word *step*. When we hear the step terms we may think of moving a step away or of distance. We may feel the step terms point us out as being different, a step removed from the ordinary. And we don't like these connotations.

Some people argue that we should no longer use the step words. They say we cannot ignore the associations with pain and loss, with folktale images, and with current-day meanings of the word *step*. We no longer need the terms, they say. Instead of saying *stepfamily,* we could use *remarried family.* Instead of *stepmother,* we could say *mother by marriage* or *my father's wife.* These people believe our feelings about our new families may improve if we change the words we use to refer to family members. Do you agree?

There are other people, however, who say that it is not necessary (and probably not possible) to completely remove the step terms from our vocabularies. The terms are useful; they give us words for our new family relationships that all people understand. Instead of getting rid of them, these people argue that we can learn new attitudes. Once we understand our reasons for not liking the step terms, they say, we can stop not liking them. The old folktales are not true, after all. They're just good stories. The pitiful *steōpcild* is of the past; today's stepchild is generally treated well. Nor do step-family members have to remain a step removed from one another or from society; they can choose where to walk and how tall to stand. It is not a change of words we need, these people argue. It is a change of attitudes.

What do you think?

But What Will Other People Say?

All young people like to feel proud of themselves and of their families. And when parents divorce, most kids worry what other people will think. They fear friends will look down on them or think them strange. When a parent remarries, they have the same kind of worries all over again.

You may have felt that, because you are a stepchild, you are different. It may seem that you are unlike most of your friends, and that your family is unusual.

There was, indeed, a time when stepfamilies were unusual. A hundred years ago, almost all families were the traditional mama, papa, baby-bear-type family. But that's no longer true.

There are millions and millions of stepfamilies today. In fact, the remarried family is only one of a great many new family types. There are also single-parent families; adoptive families; children's homes and Boy's Ranch/Girl's Town-type homes; families in which two women, or two men, choose to raise their children together; retirement homes; families without children; single-person households; collective families, in which two or more sets of parents and children share a home; and others. You may be surprised to know that there are now about as many of these new-type families as there are first-married families. That's not all. Experts predict that very soon, certainly by the year 1990, there will be more step-families and other nontraditionals than first-married families. That's right, more!

You are not alone. There are millions of other young people out there just like you. Look around your classroom at school. Out of every three people, one lives in a family that does not include both biological parents. And about one in five is a stepchild. Maybe more. Did you know there were that many? Perhaps you and they would like to locate one another.

When you tell people today that you live in a stepfamily, they aren't surprised. They already know several stepfamilies. Sometimes friends may ask questions about you and your new family relationships. But that doesn't mean they are critical, only curious. Answer their questions without self-consciousness, and you will have done them and yourself a favor.

Melanie was so nervous about what people would think at her father-daughter banquet that she felt sick. Later, she and Tammy talked about what happened. "I used to worry about people knowing George was my stepfather," Tammy said. "But it got easier every time I introduced him. I finally realized nobody pays much attention. If they don't mind, I guess I don't either!"

Don't think that just because your parent remarried, you're different. You're not, and your family is not unusual. It's just one of millions. The stepfamily is a positive and respectable life-style. Be proud of it.

WHAT ROLE SHOULD YOUR STEPPARENT PLAY?

We all know who or what a mother is and have ideas about what she's supposed to do. But what about a stepmother? Should she discipline her husband's children? Cook for them, do their dirty laundry, take them to school?

And what about a stepfather? Should he divide the money he earns equally between his first children and his step-children? Or does one or the other come first? Should he demand respect from his stepchildren? Should he make and enforce household rules? Name stepchildren in his will? Love them?

Should a stepparent be a parent?

A friend?

The question of what to call your stepparent is a question of identity: What is he or she to me? That's why it's a hard question to answer. And the answer you come up with today may not be the answer you'll like tomorrow. That's because there is no "right" answer to what a stepparent can be called or to what role he or she can play. You may have a friend who says her stepfather is just like a father to her. You may have another friend who says he hardly knows his stepmother. Stepfamilies are all different. And they work out different ways of relating.

What kind of person is your stepparent? Is he young or old? Does she have other children or has she never been married before? Is he an only child or one of ten? Does she love to cook, sew, and plant seeds, or is she more at ease before an electron microscope, at a typewriter, or among library shelves? Can he play the piano, racquetball, Monopoly? Is she quiet and shy or noisy and outgoing? And what kind of relationship does he or she hope to have with you?

The superparent. Some stepparents think they should begin, right away, to play the role of the perfect parent. For example, a woman may work very hard to see that her new stepchild wears the right clothes, eats the right foods, gets the right amount of rest, has the right kind of friends, and behaves properly at all times. Women are aware of what society expects of mothers. And some of them try too hard to prove themselves. They try to be superparents.

The rescuer. There are also stepparents who see themselves as rescuers. They believe the young person has not had the proper kind of care, love, or discipline in the past. They swoop onto the scene ready to make up for all the wrongs of the past and ready to set the new family on the right track. But they forget to ask whether the young person wants to be set on a new track.

The dictator. There are some stepparents, especially men, who feel they should have the last word on all family matters. "As long as you put your feet under my table," one father said, "you'll do what I say." This kind of person believes the best way for kids to show respect and love for parents is to obey. And he feels unloved, as well as insulted, when disobeyed. He may move into his wife's house and immediately begin giving orders. And he's almost certain to find himself in noisy fights with his stepchildren.

The reluctant parent. At the opposite extreme is the reluctant stepparent. He or she wants to make a good impression and to get along with the new stepchild, and is fearful of making mistakes and of disapproval. So instead of speaking up on matters of discipline or family management, this person is hesitant to take a stand. Because he or she does not take part in issues that concern the child, this stepparent may eventually be accused of not caring.

The cold fish. There are also stepparents who have little or nothing to do with their stepchildren. They simply have no interest in young people and no desire to have a close relationship.

There are other kinds of stepparents, too. There are those who smother their stepchildren with attention, those who ignore them, and those who are awkward in every attempt to relate. There are stepparents who are jealous of their stepchildren, and others who compete with the absent parent for the affection of the child.

Stepparents come in all sizes, shapes, and character types. There is one thing all of them have in common, however. Every single one of them fell in love with somebody else's mom or dad. That's one thing you and your stepparent have in common: You both love your parent.

Most stepparents are alike in one other way—almost all of them want to get along with their spouse's children. All too often, they just don't know how.

What kind of role does your stepparent play? What kind would you like him or her to play?

The ideal stepparent. Some young people long for a strong parent-figure who sets clear limits and enforces them. Others prefer a more casual relationship and a stepparent who remains extremely flexible. There are kids who want a stepparent who shares common interests, who likes to go places and do things with them. Still others like a stepparent who does his or her own thing allowing the young person the freedom to do the same. People are all different. The ideal stepparent for you might be an altogether different kind of person than the ideal stepparent for your best friend.

Many stepchildren say they wish their stepparent would just be a friend. Most experts agree this is best, at least in the beginning. Discipline is far easier to accept from a person who is known, trusted, and respected. This does not mean, however, that your stepparent should be goody-goody/sweet-sweet all the time. Even the best of friends have their differences. And they sometimes clash over those differences. You would not expect perfection from a friend, nor should you expect it from your stepparent. A friend is not always in a good mood. Neither is a stepparent. A friend is not without annoying habits. Neither is a stepparent. Friends don't always see eye to eye. Neither do stepparents and stepchildren. Friends sometimes have arguments. So do stepparents and stepchildren. After a fight, friends usually come back around to respecting one another's rights to be different. So can stepparents and stepchildren.

What Role Should You Play?

Just as there are many different styles of stepparenting, there are many different kinds of stepchildren. Some of them are delighted when a parent remarries. Others are disappointed. Many are angry and full of bitterness. Almost all of them, however, find that getting used to an additional parent isn't easy.

The condemner. Some stepchildren have a habit of comparing the stepparent with their absent parent. They frequently criticize and point out how much better the first parent is or was. Because the stepparent is different, they feel he or she is not as good.

The pusher. Testing is something many stepchildren do, too. They push to see what the limits are, just how badly they can behave, and just how trustworthy the stepparent is. Many deliberately bedevil a new stepparent in an attempt to cause anger. And when the stepparent does return nastiness with nastiness, the stepchild feels this is proof that the stepparent is mean or cruel.

The darling. There are other stepchildren who try always to be sweet and loving. They want and need approval and affection. And they're afraid to disagree or to speak up for their own rights. These young people need help in overcoming their insecurities. They need to learn that no one has to be perfect to be accepted and loved—even by a stepparent.

The wedge. Most kids, however, feel a stepparent is an intruder in their lives. They try to be a wedge driving the parent and stepparent apart. Or they try to prove to the parent just how bad the stepparent is in an attempt to get rid of him or her. Many play their parent's protector; they try to change how the stepparent treats the parent. Still others believe the only way they can be loyal to the absent parent is to reject the stepparent.

There are also those young people whose parents encourage or even coerce them to call their stepparent mom or dad and to act as if the stepparent were a biological parent. Some few children, mostly the very young, feel okay about treating a stepparent as a parent. But most do not. They know, deep in themselves, that the stepparent is not their biological parent. And they rebel against any efforts to make them act as if it were so.

There are other kinds of stepchildren, too. There are those who are friendly and those who are surly; those who are nice to the stepparent when their parent is looking but not so nice otherwise. And there are kids who are openly hostile at all times. Some stepchildren feel they must compete with the stepparent for the parent's attention. Others compete for their stepparent's attention. There are also those who ignore their stepparent entirely.

What kind of stepchild are you? What kind of relationship would you like to have with your stepparent?

Maybe your answer is no relationship. Maybe you don't like your stepparent. Maybe you can hardly stand him or her. That's okay. Stepparents and stepchildren don't have to love each other. They don't even have to like each other. That's right! There is no rule that says stepparents and stepchildren must like each other. No one could enforce such a rule.

What a stepparent and stepchild must do, however, is admit that they have at least one thing in common—there's someone they both want to live with, someone they both love.

You are your parent's child. You have a right to live in your parent's home. Your stepparent is your parent's husband or wife. He or she also has a right to be in your parent's home. Because your parent loves you both, each of you belongs in the family. The two of you must, therefore, learn to at least tolerate one another.

> The ideal stepchild. Some stepparents long to play the role of parent. They hope for a stepchild who will look up to them, respect them, love them. Other stepparents see themselves as simply a wife or husband and not as a parent. They wish only for affable, polite stepchildren. While one stepparent may dream of having a rough and tumble athlete to call his or her own child, another envisions having a talented musician. People are all different. The ideal stepchild for your stepparent might be an altogether different kind of person than the ideal stepchild for one of your other parents.

Relationships between stepparents and stepchildren can be close or distant, smooth or rocky, cool and businesslike, or warm and friendly. They may choose to play the roles of parent and child, good friends, or merely polite acquaintances. And they can call each other names that fit the relationships they have chosen. In fact, the nicest thing about step relationships is that they leave room for choice.

A stepparent, parent, and child are like three links in a chain. The stepparent and stepchild are connected by a common bond—the parent. Each loves and is loved by that central link. Neither has any choice over this fact. They do, however, have some other choices. They can choose to keep the chain stretched out so that the two ends never touch. They can choose to reach out to each other and form a circle. Or they can choose something in between those two extremes, touching at times, remaining more distant at others. The only inadvisable choice is to pull in opposite directions. To do so is to place great strain on that central link.

How to Get Clear on What Roles You Will Play

The best way to get your stepparent and other family members to treat you the way you'd like to be treated is to discuss the roles you play. It may seem difficult to talk about, but living day after day with unclear notions about who's who in the family is much more uncomfortable.

How do you get your family talking about these issues? You can start by choosing a time when all of you are together; mealtime is often good. Take this book to the table with you and suggest that all of you think about and then discuss the following topics:

1. *What is the relationship between you and your stepparent?*
   What does each of you expect from the other? Should you have to obey rules set by your stepparent? Should he or she have any say in how your household is run? Should you? How do you treat your stepparent—with respect, with indifference, as a friend? How does he or she treat you? How would you like to be treated?

2. *How does your parent influence your relationship with your stepparent?*
   Is your parent pushing you to call your stepparent mom or dad? Is he or she pushing the two of you to play the role of parent and child? Or does your parent stand back while

your stepparent rules the roost? Do you expect occasionally to have some time alone with your parent? Do your parent and stepparent expect occasionally to have some time alone together? Is each of you willing to allow the other this privilege?

3. Now consider your other parent, the one who (if still living) lives in another home.
Do you consider this person a part of your family? Does the parent you live with? Do you worry about what he or she thinks (or would think) of your relationship with your stepparent? Must you listen to criticism in each household about the other? Is that fair? Do you brag in either home about how the other is better? Is that fair? Are you forbidden to mention names and events with one to the other, or to have photos and other reminders of each in the other home? Would you like it if your two families got along better? Are they willing to try?

4. What about the other kids (if any) in your family?
Is there a brother or sister who tries to influence how you feel about your stepparent or what you call your stepparent? Do you try to influence another? Does your stepparent have children who live with you or come to visit? Do you consider them a part of the family? What effect do they have on your relationship with your parent? Your stepparent? Does your stepparent treat you differently when they're around? Do they try to get along with you? Do you try to get along with them?

5. Finally, discuss your feelings about your stepfamily as a whole.
Do you see yourself as a part of the family? If not, is it because you choose not to be a part or because you feel excluded? Are you invited to participate in special or fun events? In decision-making processes? In conversations?

Are there times you would especially like to be included? Are there times you would like to have the choice of participating or not without guilt? When? Are there times your parents would like you to participate that you do not? What compromises can be made?

How to Decide What Names You Will Use

Now you're ready to talk about names—what to call and be called. The names you choose are not nearly as important as how you feel about them. People are not surprised anymore to hear the terms *stepparent, stepdaughter,* or *stepson.* There are too many of us these days. But if you feel uncomfortable with using the step terms, then you can choose other terms and ask your family members to do the same.

What will you call your stepparent, and how will he or she introduce you? Some young people use two different parental terms for their parent and stepparent, such as papa and daddy, mom and mother, or father and dad. Many young people feel more comfortable, however, simply using the stepparent's first name. My teenage daughter calls my husband Jerry. My stepson refers to me as Mama-Linda and to his mother as Mama-Andra, while the youngest of our children calls her stepfather dad. Choose a name for your stepparent that feels right to you.

In families where there is a stepfather, the kids sometimes worry about last names being different. Some families solve that problem by having the stepchildren use the stepfather's last name. It's perfectly legal to do so. It's also possible to obtain a legal name change, with the biological father's permission, through a simple court procedure. Some mothers use a hyphenated last name, such as Miller-Adams, so that her relationship with both her husband and her children is shown by her name. There are also families that are comfortable with having two last names (or more). Many a mailbox today carries double or multiple last names.

Who's who in the stepfamily is not an easy question. It's one of the first that arises after remarriage and may be the most important. But if you and your family are willing to sit down and discuss roles and names together, then you have the beginning of an answer.

Chapter Four
The Stepfamily Is Different

. RON .

Ron knew it was going to be a bad day because of the way it started out. At breakfast Ron's mother (whose last name was no longer the same as Ron's) mentioned Christmas. She was thinking, she said, of asking Uncle Joe to come play Santa on Christmas morning as was the custom in the family years ago. "It's been so long since we had little ones around," she smiled.

"I'm little," Ron's sister protested. Cissy was the baby of the family for eight years until their mother remarried. Now, when their stepfather's three-year-old twin boys and his daughter, who was five, were with them, Cissy was no longer the youngest.

Ron patted his little sister's arm. "Sure you're little," he smiled. "But too big to believe in Santa."

"The twins are at the perfect age to enjoy him," Mrs. Thompson went on. "It would be such fun."

"I don't want the twins and Sherry to come on Christmas," Cissy declared. Ron and his mother exchanged glances but averted their eyes from Albert.

Cissy's stepfather put his coffee down and stared at her for a moment, then spoke to all of them. "I've been meaning to bring up the subject of Christmas," he said. "My children will be here during the week before Christmas."

"A week?" Ron's lip curled back more than he meant it to. He was only beginning to repair the damage done to his room from the last time the twins had stayed there. And the dial on his clock radio was permanently ruined.

"Yes, a week," Albert retorted. "Their mother and grandparents will pick them up Christmas morning. So we need to have our family meal and open gifts on Christmas Eve."

"We can't," Ron and Cissy said in unison. And they began babbling about Christmas morning, their own grandparents, stockings, plum pudding, the opening of gifts. A long argument followed about how Christmas is supposed to be celebrated. Cissy pointed out that Santa comes during the night so they couldn't open gifts until Christmas morning. Albert angrily reminded her that she didn't believe in Santa anyway. "So what difference does it make?" he said.

Finally, Mrs. Thompson spoke up. "The children's grandparents are accustomed to being with us for a late breakfast and the opening of gifts on Christmas morning. It's become a family tradition."

Albert's face grew red. "Are traditions more important or are people?" he said. "My kids can't be here Christmas morning; they'll be with their mother's parents. And speaking of parents, what about mine?" He looked accusingly at his wife. "You haven't said a word about inviting them. You're a Thompson now, Joyce. Is this going to be a Thompson family Christmas or not?"

"Of course it is," Joyce Thompson said. "We'll work something out."

The argument over how Christmas is supposed to be celebrated started all over again. Finally, Cissy began to cry.

"Surely this is not worth upsetting a child over," Joyce patted her daughter.

"Oh, by all means. Let's not upset *your* child," Albert rose and threw down his napkin. "There are other children in this family, you know. What about their feelings? What about mine?" There was silence for a minute. "Sometimes I wonder why I try." He stomped through the living room, snatched up his hat and coat and stormed off to work.

At dinner that evening, they all sat down together. Ron, his sister and mother had been used to coming in after school and work and eating whenever they felt hungry. But dinnertime was important to Albert; he insisted they eat together. It should be a special time of sharing and keeping in touch, he said. Ron had decided he really meant it was a good time to deliver lectures or for them to argue.

They were eating, making small talk (carefully avoiding mention of the morning's conversation), when the telephone rang.

"Hello," Albert answered.

"This is Ron's father," the voice said. "Let me speak to my son." Ed Boston had only recently moved back into town after nearly seven years in a distant city. Cissy hadn't recognized him the first time he came to their house. But she liked him. And Ron was especially enjoying getting to know his dad again.

Albert's voice was tight as he explained (for the third time that week) that they always ate dinner around seven o'clock. "Can't you call earlier or later to talk to the kids?"

"Oh, sure," Ed Boston said. "Sorry, I forgot. But I really do need to talk to Ron a minute. Put him on, would you?"

The rest of the family sat in silence while Ron talked and laughed with his Dad. They confirmed plans for Ron and Cissy to spend the weekend with Ed. "Talk to you tomorrow," Ron said and hung up.

"Hey, Cis," he ruffled his sister's hair as he sat down. "Dad said to give his best girl a hug." Joyce Thompson shifted uneasily. Both she and Ron had noticed the girl was not eating. "How about dessert?" Cissy shook her head.

"I'll get some applesauce." Ron started to get up.

"No," Albert said. "No dinner, no dessert." Ron thought his stepfather was too hard on his sister. Albert claimed Ron and his mother babied Cissy too much. "Are you going to eat your dinner or not?" Albert asked. Cissy shook her head miserably. "Then go brush your teeth and get ready for bed."

"I can get her to eat." Ron picked up Cissy's spoon.

"You can stay out of this." Albert snatched the spoon. "From now on I'd like you to leave your sister's discipline to me. Now," he said to Cissy, "go brush."

Ron felt his face flush but decided, at his mother's nod, that he'd best not interfere.

Cissy pulled herself to her feet. "I don't want to brush my teeth," she grumbled.

Ron suddenly remembered a favorite family story. "Maybe you should hide your toothbrush," he said, "under the mattress." At about four years of age, Ron had gone through a stage of hating to brush his teeth. The logical solution to his child's mind was for the toothbrush to disappear—which it did. His mother bought three new ones before she figured out what was going on, followed him from the bathroom one night, and found the cache of brushes under his mattress.

Remembering, the three of them stiffled their giggles. Not understanding their mirth, Albert glowered at them. "Go brush," he barked. Cissy slunk away.

"Say, Mom," Ron changed the subject. "Could you get me to the school by six-forty-five tomorrow night? The cast has to be there early, but you and Dad don't have to come until seven-thirty."

"Oh," Albert brightened. "Your play is tomorrow night? I've been looking forward to that." There was an awkward silence.

"He was allowed only two tickets," Joyce said.

"It's a small auditorium," Ron added quickly.

"Poor Cissy," Albert responded, "She'll be disappointed that she can't go, too. What time did you say we should be there, Ron?"

Head down, Ron said, "I was talking to Mom."

"What's that?" Albert leaned forward.

"I gave the other ticket to Dad."

"His other dad," Joyce spoke.

"Oh." Again there was silence. A long silence. Then Albert looked at his wife. "You and Ed are going together?"

"Not together. We'll just both be there."

"I suppose you expect me to think you won't be sitting together?"

"I don't know." she shrugged. "Would that bother you?"

"Bother me?" Albert rose and began to pace the floor. "Since when did you worry about what bothers *me?*" He whirled toward them. "I'll tell you what bothers me—these giggles behind my back, this insistence that Christmas be celebrated your way, which leaves out my kids, the three of you conspiring against me, and Ed, too. What bothers me is that I'm not part of this family. You won't let me be part of it, or my kids either. None of you." Albert straightened.

Ron's mother rose. "Check on Cissy for me, would you, Ron?"

Ron went. But he continued to hear voices for a long, long time, his mother begging Albert to listen, to understand, saying she loved him and her children, too. At one point, Albert said something about how she must make a choice whether she was a Thompson or a Boston. "What's it going to be, Joyce?" he kept saying. "Boston or Thompson? What's it going to be?" Ron called Cissy into his room, turned up the radio and dealt a game of hearts.

Ron and his family are having real trouble. They're having trouble partly because each of them is overly sensitive to everything that happens. They're having trouble over Ron's father's relationship with the family. And they're having trouble because Ron's stepfather feels left out. Most of all, they're having trouble feeling like a family.

FAMILY

What do you think of when you see the word *family*? Do you think of a single-parent family? A childless family? An adoptive family? A stepfamily? Probably not. You probably think of the so-called nuclear or traditional family—a father, mother, and kids. Because that's almost the only kind of family there was for so many generations, that's the kind most people still think of today. And because most of us still think that way, we cause ourselves a lot of problems.

THE FAMILY DANCE

Imagine what would happen if you and four or five other people were put on a stage before a large audience and told to do a dance together. No other instructions. No time for rehearsal. Just dance.

The music begins; the audience is waiting. You look at one another and start to move. Each tries his or her best. But your timing is off—an arm is offered here and missed there; toes are stepped on. The line is jagged, the circle never quite complete. You feel out of place, as if something were missing, as if everything were wrong. Worst of all, you're constantly aware that other people are watching every move.

Could you perform well under such circumstances? No one could. And yet we expect stepfamilies and the people in them to perform a similar feat. We expect people with different

backgrounds, different expectations, and even different opinions, who find themselves suddenly together on the stage of
one household, to begin at once to do the family dance. We
expect them to fit together as if they had been practicing for
years, to keep the same tempo and stay in step. We expect
each person to know his or her place and the group to move
as one, no matter that they have never danced together
before.

Because we and our society think of only one thing when
we hear the word *family,* we expect all families to be the same.
We expect the stepfamily to be like the traditional family.
And when it isn't, we feel disappointed, embarrassed, cheated,
angry, and defeated. We wonder why we can't get it all together—why we can't do the family dance.

The stepfamily must do a different dance from that of the
traditional family. Like the Boston/Thompson family in this
chapter, each stepfamily must learn to deal with people outside the household, work out new family traditions, and find
ways to make each member feel a part of the family.

This chapter will explain some of the ways the stepfamily is
different and how these differences can be made a part of the
stepfamily dance. Sometimes it may seem the complications
are too difficult, the participants too many, the music too
unfamiliar. But the steps can be learned. And with practice,
the stepfamily dance can be as smooth as any ever done.

LARGER AND MORE CONFUSING

The most obvious difference between the traditional family
and the stepfamily is size. A stepfamily is larger. Much larger.
Take a look at your own family. How many parents did you
have before marriage? How many have you now? How many
grandparents before? And now? How many brothers and sisters? What about aunts, uncles, nieces, nephews, and cousins?

Can you count them all without forgetting some or becoming confused? Some say that instead of a family tree, a stepfamily has a family forest!

A stepfamily is a large and complex system of relationships. And it often causes confusion. That confusion is especially frustrating for young children. One little fellow who was about to go visit his father asked if his new stepsister could come along. No, he was told, because his stepsister was not related to his father. Stamping his foot the boy said, "Who made up those rules anyway?"

Distinctions between biological and by-marriage relationships are not the only source of confusion in the stepfamily. Simply because there are so many people, vacations and family gatherings can become an ordeal. Holidays require lengthy planning—several schedules must be coordinated, difficult choices must be made about who should be included and when. And most difficult of all, it often seems that someone must be left out.

Diagrams of family trees show quite clearly how much larger and more complex stepfamilies are. The illustration of the traditional family tree shows a mother, father, two children, and their four grandparents.

The illustration of a stepfamily tree really looks like a forest. The parents in this family (Joyce and Albert) have divorced and remarried and both have children from their first marriages. Each set of children has four parents (two sets), eight grandparents (four sets), as well as two sets of siblings. If Albert or Joyce (or any of the other parents) have any children of their own after remarriage (shown in dotted lines), the family tree will become even more crowded.

Draw two diagrams of your family tree—one before and one after remarriage. Follow the examples on the next pages. Use a double line to show marriage, a double slash across these lines to show divorce, and an *X* for any family member

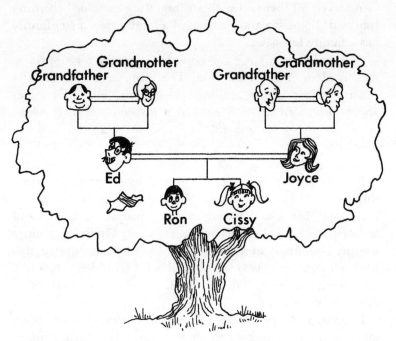

A Family Tree

who has died. Show children below and with lines descending from their biological parents.

How many new people are on your second diagram? Is there still some confusion as to who is related to whom? What would happen if you also included all aunts, uncles and cousins? Would your paper look like a battleground? When trying to get along with all these people do you sometimes feel you are on a battleground?

Many of the battles stepfamilies fight (and the pain and discomfort members often experience silently) result simply because there are a lot more people who must relate with one another. Ron must worry about his stepfather's feelings now,

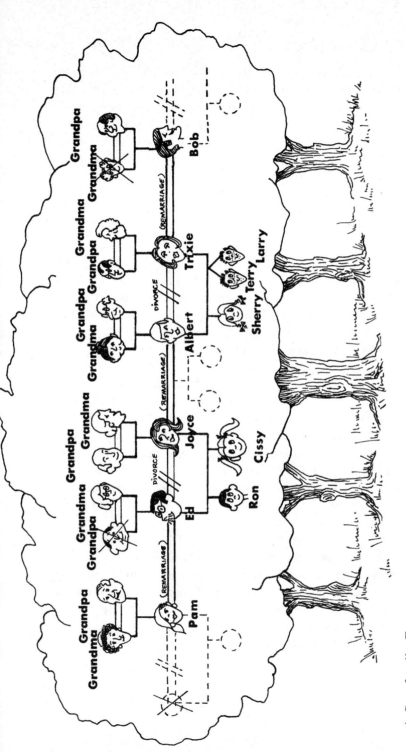

A Stepfamily Forest

as well as his father's, mother's, and stepmother's feelings. In addition to his sister, he must learn to get along with a stepsister and stepbrothers. And he must relate with other stepsiblings when he goes to his father's house. Ron's new family is like a meeting of representatives from several different countries—each of them must be quite diplomatic if they are all to get along. Even so, there is likely to be an occasional war.

There is another reason stepfamily living is much more complicated. Not only are there a lot more people, but there is a tremendously more complex pattern of relationships. For example, the illustration of the relationships in a traditional family of five shows ten pairs of relationships (counting only those within the household). Each dotted line indicates a relationship between the parents (one), each parent with each child (two through seven), and each child with every other child (eight through ten).

Now look at the illustration of relationships in a stepfamily. After divorce, just one additional person is added—a stepparent. And instead of ten relationships, there are suddenly fifteen. In this same family, if the stepparent also had a couple of kids, there would be thirty-seven relationship pairs. If a new baby arrived, the total would immediately jump to forty-six. And if there were two stepparents and both had children of their own (as in Ron's family), there would be close to one hundred relationships. In stepfamilies, relationships multiply like rabbits. And like rabbits, each must have its own space, time and nourishment to grow.

Try making a relationship diagram of your family. Draw a circle for each person. And draw dotted lines from each circle to every other circle. (It might help to use a different color pencil or crayon for each person.) Count the relationships. You may be surprised how many relationships there are just in your own household. Try adding any parents, stepparents and stepsiblings you have who live in other homes. Is it possi-

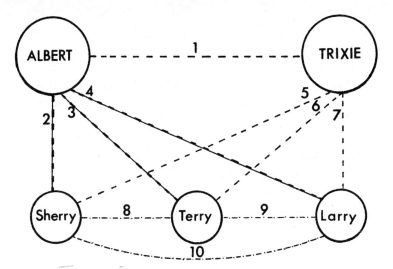

A Traditional Family of Five
Ten Relationships

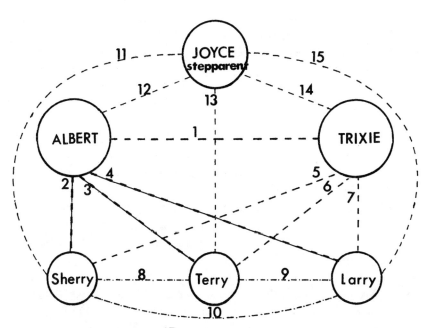

One Additional Family Member
Fifteen Relationships

ble to draw all the dotted lines without becoming confused?

The stepfamily is different. It's larger and more confusing than the traditional family. And the stepfamily dance is different from the family dance. If you and your family are having difficulty getting your act together, don't be disappointed or discouraged. There are more people, a lot more relationships, more hands reaching out in different directions, more feet to stumble over.

But the new dance steps can be learned. It just takes practice, patience, and time.

EVERYONE IS HURTING

One of the most vivid memories I have of my public school days is that of returning to school each fall and becoming so sore from the physical exercises that I was miserable. I was angry with my teachers for making me exercise, angry with my parents for making me go to school, and angry with myself for not staying in shape during the summer so I wouldn't get so sore in the fall. No matter who spoke to me or how kindly, I answered with a growl. And if someone made the mistake of touching me where I was sore, he or she was likely to be clobbered. To use my father's expression, I was like an old sore-tailed cat in a room full of rocking chairs.

The stepfamily has one major difference that is less visible than mere size. But it's just as important because it, too, affects every single relationship within the family. The difference is pain.

Stepfamily members are like old sore-tailed cats. Each has experienced a major loss in his or her life. In most cases, death or divorce has ripped away someone or something held dear. Parents lose a marriage, a spouse, an ideal. Kids lose a kind of innocence, a belief in the solidarity of their family, a parent.

Stepparents who have never been married before lose a dream, an expectation of time alone with a spouse, of sharing firsts like the birth of a child, of being the one and only.

Every single member of a stepfamily is hurting. And pain has a way of making people feel out of sorts. When in pain, the most gentle of family pets may snap at its owner or even at its own babies.

People are not so different from animals. When in pain, they're harder to get along with. And after losing a marriage, a parent, or a dream, a person is wounded. Such deep wounds take a long, long time to heal. And until they do, they're sore.

Stepfamily members have a lot of sore spots. They're angry at everyone including themselves for what has happened. Parents snap at their children. Kids fight among themselves or with adults. Stepparents get their feelings hurt and shout or pout. Everyone has a chip on his or her shoulder, and there are plenty of people around to knock it off.

There are two specific things you can do, however, to help ease the pain during the weeks and months (perhaps even years) it may take for time to work its healing magic. One is to avoid stepping on another's sore spots. If your stepfather had a sunburn and you slapped him on the back, he probably wouldn't respond with a sparkling smile. Nor would you win his favor, just after he's failed at fixing a leaky faucet, if you reminded him that your other father once installed a whole new bathroom in your house. Be sensitive to the tender spots of others. Criticize gently or not at all.

The other thing you can do is take note of your own sore spots and warn others not to tread on them. Ask your family members to be careful with you. And when you do get hurt and angry, take a look at the real cause of your pain.

You and the other members of your stepfamily have been wounded. That makes you more sensitive, defensive and vulnerable. And it makes your relationships more turbulent. But they won't always be that way. In time, you will learn to be gentle with one another.

Us Versus Them

If you came home from a ball game at your school and said, "We won," who would you mean? Probably not just the ball team. Instead you'd have drawn an imaginary circle in your mind around your entire school—students, teachers, staff, everyone who supports the team. By using the word *we,* you placed yourself inside the circle. You belong.

All people have the need to belong. That's one reason they all make imaginary circles in their minds—around themselves and their schools, churches, clubs, and other organizations. And because of these imaginary circles, people tend to think in terms of *us* and *them.* Our circles help us feel we belong.

A sense of belonging does not happen overnight, however. If you've ever moved to a new school you know that imaginary circles, though invisible, are very strong. It may have taken a long time to erase the old circle and to be drawn into a new circle of friends.

Family members draw imaginary circles too—family circles. In a traditional family the circle is nice and simple. It includes all the people in the household—everyone agrees.

But in a stepfamily the imaginary circle is not so simple. In fact, the circles in the minds of all the different family members frequently disagree. For example, in a young person's mind, the original family circle often remains as clearly drawn as ever, in spite of divorce or death. A stepmother may include her husband's children in her circle, while they are not yet ready to include her in theirs. A stepfather may feel guilty about drawing a circle around his wife's children, since his own children cannot live with him. Kids usually include the parent who lives outside the home in their circles, while parents often pressure their children to erase that portion of the picture. And kids who are in a parent's home only on weekends or in the summer are often confused as to how or whether they fit into that other family circle. And so are their parents. In the stepfamily there is a lot of confusion as to where the family circle ends and where it begins.

Stop reading for a minute and imagine what it would be like to move from your present school to another. Then imagine attending a ball game between teams from both schools. Who would be *us*, in this situation, and who *them?* To which imaginary circle would you belong?

At ball games it may seem necessary to decide which side to be on, which team to cheer. But in families, thinking in terms of us versus them causes trouble. A lot of the problems in stepfamilies are caused by just this us-versus-them syndrome.

One of the most troublesome issues is territory—is this my place or yours? Are you invading my turf or am I in your way? Instead of the house being ours, some members feel it's theirs because they lived in it first. They resent the newcomers. And the newcomers resent being made to feel they don't belong.

The most difficult of all the us-versus-them issues is having to share the people we love. A four-year-old who found her stepbrother sitting on her father's lap demanded that he get off. "He's my daddy, not yours," she said. Like most children in stepfamilies, this child was upset at having to share her parent's love.

People also become upset when they feel excluded. Ron's stepfather was distressed by a common problem—in a stepfamily, the parent and child, or children, have been together much longer than the stepparent has been with them. As a result, a stepparent may sometimes feel like an outsider, like he or she doesn't belong. In other situations, it's the young person who feels left out because the parent and stepparent have an intense new relationship. Or a parent may feel excluded if the child and the stepparent become close friends. The children in a stepfamily may form an alliance, too, from which one or more children are excluded. Whenever three or more people get together in a stepfamily, someone is likely to feel that a circle has been drawn which excludes him or her.

The sense of not belonging is one of the most lonely and painful of all human emotions. But is there anything stepfamilies can do about the us-versus-them syndrome? Is there any way to help everyone feel as if he or she belongs?

Yes. There are some things that help.

One of the most important is to talk about your imaginary circles. Sit down together with paper and pencil and let each family member draw his or her circle. Is there someone you'd rather not include? Is there someone who would rather exclude you? People are sometimes afraid to admit these kinds of feelings. But it helps when they know that all stepfamily members sometimes feel this way. And when there is more openness among family members, there is a far greater chance that each person can be made to feel that his or her feelings are important. Each person matters. Each belongs.

Another helpful device is to become aware of the kinds of terms you use. Do you often speak of us and them, ours and theirs, yours and mine? When you say *we*, who exactly do you mean? And what about the home you share? Do you think of it as belonging to all of you or only to some? How do other family members feel? It's a good idea for a stepfamily to start out in a new house or apartment so that no one is the outsider or the intruder, no feeling of the space being *mine* or *yours*. Instead, the house is *ours*.

Sometimes it's not possible to move into a new home, however. In that case, it's helpful for all family members to discuss the use of space. Each person needs some space that is his or her very own even if it's only a closet, a drawer, or a box that is safe against violation. Squabbling over turf diminishes when all have agreed on how the household space will be used, when, and by whom. And cooperation in the use of space can, in itself, help create a sense of family unity.

There are other things that can be done as well. Stepfamily members can begin to do things together in different groups. A stepfather and stepchild might go out to dinner or a movie together, for example. Or a stepmother might take her step-daughter shopping. Members from the two different original families might look for interests they could share, hobbies they could enjoy together. When people relate on a one-to-one basis, they generally communicate more honestly and find it easier to like one another. And one-to-one relationships are far less complicated than the spaghetti-bowl confusion of family relating.

Stepfamilies can also plan special events which include everyone. A good meal, music, candlelight, and personal invitations to share good times can help induce a sense of togetherness. Most importantly, stepfamily members can remember, when the us-versus-them syndrome is rampant, that times change. People change. With a little time and with practice, the stepfamily dance can be done.

OUTSIDE INTERFERENCE

As if there weren't enough troubles within the household, the stepfamily must also deal with interference from outside. Grandparents and other relatives may increase tension with inequitable gift-giving or by ignoring the new stepchildren altogether. Still others, fearful of being unfair, may overcompensate, pay more attention to the newcomers, and cause the original children to feel left out and jealous. Just as step-family members struggle with the question of what roles they should play in the new family, relatives and friends outside the household are also confused.

If things said or done by other relatives or friends make you uncomfortable, speak up. Let them know how you feel. But also be ready to try to understand their feelings and confusion. In time, they will probably become more comfortable with your family situation and less troublesome. In time, they too will understand the stepfamily dance.

There is another person outside your household who affects relationships within—your other parent. Many parents feel threatened by the appearance of a new parenting figure in their child's life.

One man called his children much more often after their stepfather came into the family. He made a point of asking for "my daughter," or "my son," and seemed to enjoy the awkwardness his visits caused. He also made a point of inviting the children out at times when he knew their other family had special plans. Like Ron's father, he deliberately interferred with his children's becoming part of their new family.

A young friend of mine once mentioned his mom (meaning his stepmother) when he was with his biological mother. Angrily, she informed him that she, not "that other woman," was his mom. And she told him never to refer to his stepmother as mom again. This woman deliberately tried to prevent her son and his stepmother from having a close relationship.

Parents interfere in other ways, too. Some say nasty things about the other parent or stepparent. Some try to control how the child is disciplined in the other home. Or they may use the young person as a spy or messenger and ask questions or send angry messages back and forth.

Stepparents sometimes act this way too. One stepfather succeeded (with his wife's help) in convincing his young stepchildren that their father was a terrible person not worthy of their affection. He pressured them into refusing to visit their father all through their growing-up years. It wasn't until they were adults that they discovered their father was a likable—even lovable—person.

Such parents often think they are doing their children a favor by protecting them from a person they consider undesirable. But recent studies show that a child benefits from continued contact with both biological parents no matter what those parents are like.

It's not hard to understand why parents and stepparents behave in these ways. They've lost a home, a marriage, a dream; they're fearful of losing something more—a child. Their situation is very similar to the age-old problem of sibling rivalry—each child in a family is jealous of every other child, each is afraid the other will receive more attention or love, and each dreams of having the parents only to himself or herself. But every child learns to live with these feelings. And most conclude that the advantages of having brothers and sisters outweigh the disadvantages.

Parents and stepparents sometimes come to a similar conclusion. They discover that a stepparent is not a replacement for a parent—only an additional parent. They learn that a young person can like, even love, more than one set of parents. Lucky is the young person whose parents all know that having more than one set of parents doesn't cause a child to love them any less.

What about your family? Does it suffer from outside interference? In what way do your parents' and stepparents' attitudes toward one another color your feelings toward them? You don't have to like or dislike a person just because a member of your family does. You can make your own decisions.

If your parents say bad things about each other, come right out and tell them it hurts to hear someone you love criticized. If they ask about your other parents' habits, tell them you are uncomfortable talking about the other people's private lives. If they make a practice of sending messages through you (other than information about when you'll be picked up or brought back home), ask them to tell the other person them-selves. Children should not be used as weapons or caught in the middle of their parents' fights.

You have the right to a relationship with both biological parents. You have the right to love both. Stand up for those rights. Ask your parents to read this section. Ask them to give you the gift of permission to enjoy both homes.

What other things can you and your remarried family do about outside interference? Many times, you can ignore it. If new grandparents give your stepsibling nicer gifts than they give you (or give you none at all), just remember that gifts are not reflections of how good or bad a person you are. The unequal gift giving means only that the grandparents have known your stepsibling longer than you. And they have not yet gotten used to the idea that you too are now a part of their family. You can also remember that you have other relatives, who probably do things for you that they don't al-ways do for your stepsibling. The fact is, remarried families don't share all the same relatives. So there simply are going to be some differences in visitation schedules, in gifts, and in other types of opportunities.

ADVANTAGES OF LIVING IN A STEPFAMILY

It's true, the stepfamily is different. It's more complicated than a traditional family. But different doesn't mean worse—only different. And there are some great advantages to living in step.

One of them is having more people who can come to care for you and be interested in you. You may have two sets of parents, four sets of grandparents, several siblings, and a whole gang of cousins, aunts, and uncles. From this wide range of people, there are some you can become friends with, some you can count on when you need help, and some you may come to love. Many stepchildren grow to feel so much a part of a stepparent's family that they forget they were not actually born into that family. One young man went to work for his stepgrandfather and became a partner in the business.

There are other advantages to having more people around. You will almost certainly have more opportunities for different kinds of experiences, more vacations, and other special events. One girl, listening to her friends recount their summer activities said, "I feel deprived. All my friends get to go more places and do more things because they have more parents!"

When you have two sets of parents, you also have two sources of help when it comes time to find a costume for the school play, buy a band instrument, learn to fix your own hair, pay for a college education, play a game of cards, or purchase a car. More is sometimes better. Even when it comes to parents.

There are other less tangible benefits to living in step. A remarried home may become more stable both financially and emotionally than before the remarriage. Not only that, a parent who is happy in a new relationship has more to give his or her child than a parent who is lonely or unhappy.

There's at least one more important advantage for you. People learn to have good marriages by witnessing good marriages. You can learn from watching your parent and stepparent relate just how it is two people who love one another can work out their differences. (And people always have differences no matter how much they love each other.) As you share in the daily ups and downs, joys and sorrows, play and work, laughter and tears of this new marriage, your life can be enriched in a way that will be important for your future.

Living in step is not a bed of roses. But it's not just a bunch of thorns either. It's both. So when you're getting stuck by some thorn just remember, there'll be blossoms too.

Chapter Five
Illusions of Hell and Paradise

. ERIC .

Eric helped himself to another piece of his little sister's birthday cake and headed for his room. The cake was a garish, ugly thing covered with bright pink and green roses, nothing like the pretty pastel cakes his mom once baked. His stepmother, Norma, bought it at a bakery. Norma never did anything the way his mom used to. But his mom would never bake him another cake. Eric's mom was dead.

"That you, Eric?" Norma called from the other room.

"Into the cake again are you?" Eric's father winked at his wife. They sat with glasses of wine in the living room talking about how much the children enjoyed the day. "Mandy's birthday party was terrific," Bill told Norma. "You're a great mom."

Norma smiled. She really did try hard with the children. And it was paying off. Little four-year-old Tammy stuck to her like glue. And Mandy seemed to be warming up a little though she was so quiet it was hard to tell. Eric, Bill's teenager, was a little tougher; he still objected when the girls called Norma mom. But Norma had read that older kids are slower to accept a stepparent. She felt sure she was winning him over, too.

"I think we did the right thing in removing all the old reminders of another life," Norma said. "It's best for the children to leave the past behind and live in the present."

Bill nodded though he still felt a little uneasy about their decision to destroy all reminders of his ex-wife. He couldn't get over the look on Eric's face as they tore up the photo of Erica the boy kept on his dresser. Bill knew Eric had another photo in his billfold; he didn't have the heart to take it, too. But Norma would be angry if she found out. Maybe she was right. Maybe allowing the kids to dwell on their memories was unhealthy.

"When the adoption goes through," he said, "that will seal the kid's place in the present and make us all feel more secure."

"I can hardly wait," Norma beamed, "to tell them I'm going to be their real mom."

"And such a good one." Bill was remembering Erica and her drinking. Toward the last he found her drunk at the end of every day. At any rate the kids had a good life now. "To our family." They raised their glasses and drank.

From his room, Eric heard a strange sound like a muffled sob. He went to the room his sisters shared and found Mandy crying.

"Hey, what's the matter?"

"I don't know," Mandy confessed. Eric stroked her hair while she tried to explain through her sniffles that she'd had a great day, wonderful presents, a delicious cake. But something was wrong. She felt sad. And she felt guilty without knowing why.

"You're missing Mom, aren't you," Eric said. Mandy turned her face to the wall and broke into fresh sobs.

Eric was twelve when their mother died. Her car went spinning into the concrete buttress of a highway bridge. Rumor said it was suicide. It happened more than a year ago, but Eric and his sisters hadn't seen their mother for a couple of years before that. She had been in a hospital. Tammy and Mandy knew only that she was sick. But Eric questioned his father about it. "She never pulled out of the depression after Tammy's birth," he explained. "She was depressed after you came, and even more so after Mandy. But when little Tammy was born it was as if she fell in a black hole and could never crawl out again."

That was his whole explanation of Erica's illness. But Eric believed there was more to it than that. In fact, he was sure the real cause was Norma.

Bill and Norma had been friends for years. They met in law school. After graduating, Norma and Bill went to work for the same law firm. Later, Eric could remember this part, the two of them bought an old house, redecorated it, and opened their own law office—Bascom and Bailey it was called then. Now it was Bascom and Bascom; Norma and Bill married right after Erica's death.

Eric's pain rose to the surface but he pushed it down. He must be strong to comfort Mandy. Tammy awakened and asked what was wrong. "Nothing," Eric patted the four-year-old. "Go back to sleep." But Eric really believed everything was wrong. He and his sisters could never have a normal life now. They lived under a shadow. It was not just their mother's death. What was even worse was that they had to live with the woman who was responsible. Norma had purchased new furniture, new dishes; she repainted and rearranged everything in the house. Eric believed she destroyed their mother and was now bent on destroying all evidence she ever existed. Well, she couldn't do it. He was determined to remain loyal to his mother. Eric's memories of his mom flourished even in what he felt was the desert of their lives.

"Don't cry, Sissy." Little Tammy crawled in bed with her sister. "We have a new mommy now." Eric flinched.

Their father appeared in the doorway. "What's the matter?"

"Mandy wants our old mommy back," the innocent voice rang out.

"No I don't," Mandy started. She thought her father would be angry if he knew she missed her mother after Norma had done so much for her birthday.

"What made you think of Erica?" Norma was right behind Bill. "Have you been pumping her full of ideas again?"

"No," Eric whirled. "I was trying to comfort her. Don't blame me for what you caused."

"What do you mean?" Bill asked.

"Nothing," Eric turned away.

"What is it, Eric?" Norma said. "You're really upset, aren't you?" She touched his shoulder, he jerked and started for the door. "Wait, Eric," Norma caught his arm. "You're always running away from me. I could help you if you'd let me."

"Sure," he said. "Like you helped my mother?" Eric was sorry as soon as the words were out. His father and Norma both started in on him. What exactly did he mean? Why wouldn't he let go of the past? Life was so much better now. Why did he insist on influencing his sisters against Norma?

"I really want to be your mother," Norma said. "Is there something I could do, something I could change that would make you like me better?"

"Yeah," Eric gave Norma an icy stare. "You could leave."

Mandy and Tammy were both sobbing now. Norma slumped into a chair and began to wipe her own tears. His father stomped about the room. "Eric, why are you doing this? Why are you attacking those who love you? I know you miss your mother. The girls miss her too. Mandy does, anyway; Tammy can hardly remember Erica. But missing your mom is no excuse for upsetting your little sisters like this. And poor Norma, she's just an innocent bystand—"

"Poor Norma!" Eric blurted. "She's the one who caused all

this. Mom would never have had to go away if it hadn't been for her fooling around with you."

Norma's eyes widened. "That's not true, Eric. Your mom was sick long before I became your father's . . ."

"Long before we became friends," Bill finished.

"Friends? Ha!" Eric scoffed. "If friends was all you were, Mom wouldn't be dead to . . ." A crash ended Eric's sentence. His father stood trembling with his hand drawn back.

"Apologize." Bill demanded.

"Apologize for telling the truth?" Eric shook his head.

"Wait," Norma said. "This arguing won't help. But I want to tell you something, Eric, that may help. Is it all right if I tell them now, Bill?"

"Whatever you think," he shook his head.

"It's a surprise for all of you."

"What? What?" the girls wanted to know.

"I want all of you to know how much I care about you. Eric, I want you to be mine. I've filed legal adoption papers."

"No."

"What's adoption?" little Tammy asked.

"That means Norma's going to be your real mommy," Bill said.

"No," Eric croaked. "She could never be our mother. Mother was good and kind. She was beautiful and . . ." Eric darted out of the room.

All people dream. They have fantasies and illusions. But people who live in stepfamilies often have more unrealistic dreams than most. Some look back on a paradise that never really existed as they remember it. Others imagine themselves in a living hell. Or they fantasize a perfect kind of family life that cannot exist. Because of their unrealistic mental images, stepfamily members often suffer a great deal of pain and unhappiness.

Eric dreamed of a wonderful time before his mother's death and imagined life could never be good again. He believed his stepmother was to blame for all he'd lost. His parents dreamed of wiping out all the pain of the past. And they longed for a perfect future, believing adoption could bring happiness. Kids whose parents have divorced often dream of their parents getting back together. And most stepfamily members fantasize events and feelings they never talk about. This chapter will help you understand some of the most common stepfamily illusions.

WHO'S TO BLAME

One of the illusions that haunts stepfamily members has to do with blame. My mother tells a story about an incident that happened when I was a toddler being potty trained. My cousin Jerry and I were playing together one afternoon when my mother noticed a puddle at my feet. Seeing her anger, I quickly exclaimed, "No, Mommy, not me. Jerry did it!"

Very early in life we learn to blame. Whenever a dish is broken, a finger mashed, or a car wrecked, we ask who did it? So when a divorce occurs, the question who's to blame almost always arises. Young people often blame one parent or the other. Family friends sometimes choose sides. And parents may encourage one-sided loyalty too, each portraying the other as the villain and himself or herself as the victim. Unfortunately, the divorce laws of many states contribute to this kind of blaming, too. They often require that one partner be proven guilty and the other innocent. In our society it seems divorcing parents are expected to be enemies.

Instead of blaming their parents, however, many kids feel they themselves are the cause of their family's troubles. Even when a parent has died, some kids feel they're responsible, perhaps because in a moment of anger they had a fleeting wish that the parent were dead. Self-blame sometimes becomes so intense that a young person runs away or considers suicide.

Stepparents often find themselves targets of blame too. If a stepparent and parent were friends before the divorce or death, like Bill and Norma, the stepparent will almost certainly be suspected or blamed. Some kids believe their stepparent is entirely at fault. Others blame both the stepparent and their remarried parent. They try to get back at the two by attempting to cause trouble between them. Blame plays an important role in almost all stepfamily situations. And it always causes pain and unhappiness.

Who's to blame is the wrong question to ask in stepfamily situations. If you, like Eric, believe your stepparent or some other person caused the break-up of your parents' marriage, let go of that blame. Divorce always has many causes, not just one. A new relationship sometimes hastens the ending of a marriage. But it is never the one and only cause.

If you feel angry with the parent who moved or asked for the divorce, let go of that blame. It may seem as if one parent is guilty and the other innocent. But there is more than one side to every story. When disagreements occur, it's simply because people have different opinions. No one is to blame.

If you have felt some guilt since your parents' marriage ended, let go of that self-blame. You were not the cause. Wishing a person dead cannot cause him or her to die. Neither can a child cause a divorce. Kids are often at the center of their parents' disputes, especially during the stormy last months before divorce. But that does not mean the kids caused the conflict. It means only that both the parents love the child, and they were fearful of what would happen to the parent-child relationship if divorce occurred. Parents do not divorce because of anything their children do, but because they no longer want to be married to each other.

Like dead grass in a winter lawn, blame stifles new growth. It clogs relationships with anger and frustration. In holding on to blame, stepfamily members stay stuck in an unproductive tangle of hostility. They prevent themselves from making a new beginning.

Our society is finally beginning to recognize the fact that blame is destructive in family divorce. Some states now have "no-fault" divorce laws that allow families to separate in a cooperative atmosphere rather than in one of hostility. And some churches now offer a ceremony for families who are divorcing—a way to make it formally known that the family will no longer live as a single unit, and that no one is to blame.

The past is past and cannot be changed. Blaming either yourself or someone else for what has happened in the past will not help you live through today. Nor will it bring back yesterday.

THE GHOST OF THE DEAD OR ABSENT PARENT

If one of your parents has died or gone away, you know how hard it was for Eric. You know how much Mandy and Tammy missed their mother even though they couldn't remember her very well. You know how painful death and separation are for those who are left behind.

A young person whose parent has died or gone away has many problems to work through. He or she may sometimes feel sad, lonely, angry, depressed, or all of these at once. Some kids worry whether the other parent might also go away. And some are frightened of dying, too.

It's only natural to have all these feelings. Dr. Elisabeth

Kubler-Ross, a specialist in the field of death and dying, wrote about the kinds of feelings we have about loss:

Denial. When we first learn that a person we love has died or left, we are likely to deny that fact and pretend it isn't true. "No. Not my father!" is a typical response. For the young person who is still denying the fact of a parent's death, relating with a stepparent is very difficult.

Anger. Another of the feelings most people have is anger. "Why me? Why my mother?" We may be angry with the person who abandoned us, or we may blame another person for the death (a doctor, the other parent, a stepparent, God, or ourselves). We may feel angry with different people at different times. But we're sure to feel that there is nothing fair about death.

Regret. A third response to the pain of loss may be to focus on the "ifs." If I had been better, would my parent still be here? If my mother had treated my father better, would my father still be here? In effect, we try bargaining to see if there is some way to make things go back like they were before.

Depression. Once we realize things will never be the same, depression sets in. We cry. We feel sad. We believe we can't go on without this person we loved so much. Because we know life will never be the same, we feel it will never be good again.

Acceptance. Finally, however, most of us work through the other feelings and eventually come to an acceptance of loss. We stop denying what is real. We find that anger and blaming do not bring back the person we love, nor do they ease the pain. We stop trying to find ways to change what has happened. And we set aside depression, knowing that life must go on. We even learn that life can be good again— not the same, of course. Nonetheless, it can be good.

If your parent has died, you have, no doubt, had many of these feelings, maybe all of them. It's easiest to work through painful feelings if you talk about them with someone you trust, like a parent. But many parents are uncomfortable in conversations about death or about a person who has died. If you find your parent reluctant or unwilling to allow you to talk about your dead parent and your feelings, then you should look for someone else to talk with, a minister, counselor, other family member or a good friend.

Some parents, like Eric's, feel threatened by reminders of a dead parent. They remove photos and other mementoes of the dead person and avoid mentioning his or her name. They don't mean any harm of course; perhaps they think if they ignore the fact that there once was another parent, then the stepfamily can function just like a traditional family. Perhaps they think you and your stepparent will get along better this way.

If your parents seem to be acting this way, what they probably don't know is that it is important for you to be allowed to remember and refer to your dead parent. He or she was an important part of your life, and still is. Refusing to mention that part of your past life will not make it go away. In fact, refusing to talk about events can only cause you to remember them in a hazy way and possibly unlike they really were.

People have a tendency, in looking back over their lives, to remember only the good times. Kids who lose a parent tend to recall only the fun events and warm moments with that parent. They forget the faults and eventually come to think of the dead or missing parent as having been marvelously wonderful—the perfect saint.

No one is perfect. Such memories are only that—memories.

Life with that parent had its ups and downs, and still would have if he or she had lived. Memories are nice. But they aren't real. They are illusions of our own making.

I had a friend whose father died when we were quite young. We spent a lot of time together before her father's death and continued to be close for years afterward. I found it very curious to compare her memories of her father with mine.

As I saw it, he was a harsh, cruel man. He yelled at his children continually and often hit them and their mother, leaving ugly bruises. He drank a lot. And there always seemed to be beer in the house even when there wasn't any milk. The man also had a good side, of course. A few times he took Jana, my friend, with him to work. He sometimes allowed her to help him with a project he was working on in the garage. Jana loved those occasions, and it was those she chose to remember. The longer the time since his death, the more fondly she seemed to remember him.

Not many parents are as harsh and cruel as Jana's dad. But none of them are perfect either. Parents are not angels; they're people. And people have faults.

If one of your parents is dead, or far away, you may find yourself dreaming a lot about how different your life would be if he or she were still around. And, of course, it would be very different. But dreams about *what might have been* are wasted dreams. They can only get in the way of *what can be,* under current circumstances. Living in the past can only be painful. There comes a time when we must let go of our fantasies and move on to deal with life as it now exists.

I'm not suggesting that you try to forget your dead or absent parent. On the contrary, keep your photographs, mementoes and sweet memories. They are invaluable. Neither am I saying that you should accept your stepparent as a replacement. One person cannot replace another.

But there is a chance your stepparent can become someone

special to you. Your life may be richer because of your relationship.

If you've ever thought or said to your stepparent, "My real dad (or mom) would never treat me this way," then think about that claim. Is it fair for you to expect one person to be the same as another? Comparing one person with another is never helpful in relationships.

Look at the situation from another view: Would you have treated your "real" parent the same way you treat your stepparent? Do you show him or her the same kind of courtesies and affection?

Instead of saying or thinking, "My real parent would never have treated me this way," try thinking about and saying how you would like to be treated now, today. Let your stepparent know, politely, what you like and what you don't like. Find out how he or she likes to be treated, as well. Or try this experiment. For one whole twenty-four-hour period, treat your stepparent like a friend or guest. Speak politely, gently. Say please and thank you. And show genuine concern for his or her interests and feelings. Try treating your stepparent as if you liked him or her. And see how you are treated in return. It might be a valuable experiment for both of you.

Remember your parent who is gone. But don't let the ghost of that parent (created in your mind) stand between you and the new adult who has come into your life. Your lost parent wouldn't want that to happen. The relationship you had with that parent is one thing; it still lives in your memory and is an important part of your life. But the relationship with your stepparent is something else. It's okay to have both. Both can enrich your life.

Is Adoption Good or Bad?

Some parents, like Eric's, dream of adoption. They believe the stepparent and stepchild will be closer if bound by law.

Most of all, they hope the family will be unified and the members feel complete or whole.

But families that go through adoption for these reasons are disappointed. They discover that adoption, in and of itself, cannot create family closeness. Some stepfamilies eventually do develop a strong sense of family unity. The stepparent and stepchildren come to love one another just as much as biological parents and their children do. But adoption isn't the reason. The natural growth of feelings over a long period of time is the reason. Feelings cannot be changed by signatures on paper.

Adoption can also be unfair. Parents may think they can erase the past with adoption. Or they may believe the child would be better off if there were no further contact with the parent who lives outside the home. But asking a young person to deny an essential part of his or her past is asking the impossible. It only prolongs the pain. Many an adopted child has, as an adult, gone in search of the biological parent. Each of us seems to have a built-in need for connection with our past. Adoption does not obliterate that need. One woman who went in search of her father found he was, indeed, an irresponsible drunk as her mother had always said. "But it is my mother whom I resent," she explained, "because there was another side to my father also."

There are times when adoption is what everyone in the family wants. Some stepparents wish to show their love and commitment to their stepchildren in a formal way. They want to secure their own legal rights as the parent, and they want to secure legal rights for the children. Some kids like the idea of adoption too. They feel reassured by the stepparent's desire to be officially the parent. And they like taking the stepparent's name as their own.

But families that go through the adoption process expecting it to cement family relationships will find they were dreaming an unrealistic dream. Adoption is merely a legal process; it alone cannot change attitudes or feelings.

WISHING PARENTS WOULD GET BACK TOGETHER

One of the dreams all children of divorced parents have is that their parents will eventually get back together. Even after remarriage, some young people try to make this dream come true. They set up situations that will cause their parents to have to be together, believing that if the parents see or talk to each other, they will remember how much in love they were and will want to get together again. Such plans work only in the movies. In real life they generally backfire, and the young people who make the plans usually end up witnessing just one more argument instead.

Another dream all stepchildren have is that of getting rid of the new stepparent. Some openly admit plotting against Dad's new wife or Mom's husband. The reasons are not hard to understand. Every stepchild has experienced loss—the loss of a parent through divorce or death, the loss of a part of the self, the loss of the sense of being whole. Remarriage and the appearance of a stepparent are reminders of those painful losses. Since none of us likes pain, we wish to be rid of such reminders.

It is not evil or bad to wish your stepparent were not there. There isn't a person alive who hasn't, at some time, wished another person out of the way or even dead. You are not a bad person if you have such fantasies.

The problem with these kinds of dreams, however, is that they get in the way.

Getting rid of your stepparent will not bring your parents back together. Divorced parents are a lot like Humpty Dumpty. No one else can put them back together again, not all the king's horses or all the king's men. And neither can you. About the best you can do is to let go of that old dream of a family reunion. It would be nice if parents never divorced. But they do. It would be nice if kids could help their parents get back together again. But they can't. It would be nice if all good dreams came true. But they don't. In fact, what often results from a stepchild's efforts to get rid of a stepparent is not the realization of a dream at all but a nightmare instead. An attempt to prevent two people who care about each other from being together can only cause anger, hostility, and pain for everyone.

Continuing to dream of a family reunion can be disruptive in another way. It can prevent you from allowing a relationship to develop between you and your stepparent. He or she will never replace your other parent—mothers and fathers are not replaceable; they're forever. But your stepparent just may be an interesting person to know. He or she may have something to offer you in the way of friendship, companionship, or support. You may become part of a new and larger family unit composed of many people who care about you, people who can help you through the process of healing old wounds, people who can help you again feel whole.

SILENT WISHES CAN'T COME TRUE

Have you ever looked forward to a special event such as Christmas or a birthday only to be disappointed when it didn't turn out the way you hoped it might? Have you ever dreaded something such as a dentist appointment or a big exam only to find that it wasn't nearly as bad as you'd imagined? We often expect things to turn out differently than they actually do. Then we feel unsettled or disappointed because of the difference between our expectations and reality.

Every single member of a stepfamily has some expectations about what life will be like together or about what family life should be like. Often each is expecting something very different from what others are expecting. But it seldom occurs to them to talk about their fantasies. And it's when that happens, when their dreams and expectations differ without their knowing it, that problems arise. Consider family vacations, for example.

Suppose you and your family decided to take a trip. You've agreed that each of you would go, and that each would do his or her part of the planning and packing. So you each went on your way to do just that.

Now you're in the car. But something's wrong. One member wore a swimsuit and a straw hat. She anticipated traveling to the sea shore, building a sandcastle and lying in the sun. But another of the family dressed in ski pants, sweater, and boots. Snow-covered mountain slopes were in this person's dreams. Still another purchased tickets to Disneyland, Marineworld and the San Diego Zoo, while a fourth charted a course to the most famous theaters, museums, and art shows. Alas, the fifth family member purchased a fishing license and packed all her fishing gear.

Each is prepared for a wonderful vacation. But each is doomed to frustration because expectations were not talked about. The longed-for vacation may end before it ever had a real chance to begin.

Stepfamilies often embark on the voyage of living together in much this same haphazard way. Each has a vision in his or her own head as to what "family life" should be like. Each prepares silently. And each looks forward to or dreads certain aspects of the journey. Then they set out; and each is disappointed when they don't arrive at the dreamed-of seashore, mountaintop, or amusement park.

What kind of family life did you expect when your parent remarried? Did you dream of happiness? Did you imagine it would be hell?

Young people have expectations about how a parent is supposed to act. One young fellow I knew believed that fathers are supposed to take you fishing. And he was disappointed when his new stepfather didn't do so. Actually, his stepfather was an office worker who'd never been fishing and didn't know how. Neither did he know his stepson wanted to go fishing. If the two had talked about the boy's expectations, perhaps they could have agreed to try fishing or to do something else they both would have enjoyed. As it was, the boy felt cheated and the stepfather felt like a failure in his inability to make friends with his stepson.

In another case, a girl looked forward to her father's remarriage and envisioned bringing friends home from school to be greeted with warm chocolate-chip cookies and milk. Trouble was, the lady her father married didn't like to cook. In fact, she seldom ever set foot in the kitchen, though she had other talents and interests to share with her family. But the girl felt cheated and angry because she had believed that mothers are supposed to stay at home and bake chocolate-chip cookies for their children.

All stepfamily members have expectations. A mother may expect that remarriage will be a magic cure for all her troubles, her loneliness, her financial worries, and her parenting difficulties. Both parents may expect that each will love the other's children instantly and that the children will love in return. A father may think that his new wife, who has never had children before, will just automatically know how to mother his children. A stepchild sometimes expects the new stepparent will suddenly make him feel whole again, repairing all the old unhappiness and damage of the past.

Do you have some beliefs about what mothers and fathers are supposed to be like and what they are supposed to do? Does your stepmother have some ideas about how children are supposed to behave? Does your stepfather believe you should treat him a certain way? What kind of expectations do each of you have about how your family should function and how you should relate?

Unless you and your family discuss your dreams, you may find yourselves on a chaotic journey for which none of you is properly prepared.

A good way to begin sharing expectations is to choose one topic at a time to discuss. Be sure everyone has a chance to be heard. Perhaps you might begin with what mothers are supposed to be like and what they are supposed to do. The next evening you might talk about fathers and the next about children. Finally, you might discuss what a family is and what families are supposed to do. It is important to remember that there are no "correct" answers. Each of us has his or her own ideas and beliefs; all of them are valid. The purpose of talking is not to force anyone to change, but to allow each family member to be heard and understood.

Silent wishes can't come true. But compromises can be made if dreams are shared. Mom can swim at the seashore on the way to Joey's Disneyland. Dan can visit the museum while Lila goes fishing. And Tom can ski on the way home. Just because dreams are different doesn't always mean they are incompatible. But they certainly cannot be fulfilled unless they are talked about.

Examine the illusions in your head. And ask your family members about their visions. Do some of you still harbor blame, silent wishes, fantasies of a family reunion? Do you (or your parents) believe adoption will change your lives? Do you allow memories to prevent you from living today?

Eric, his father, and his stepmother all had false illusions. Eric became friends with Norma only after he stopped blaming her and idealizing his mother. Norma won her stepchildren's affection only after she quit competing with their mother and allowed the kids their natural sense of grief over losing her. She and Bill also had to let go of their belief that their stepfamily could function like a traditional family. But it took several crises, like the one at the beginning of this chapter, for all of them to recognize and dispel all their illusions of hell and paradise that kept getting in the way.

Do you and your family members have unrealistic dreams? Can you talk about them? Can you sit down and chart a course together toward a journey you'd be willing to share? Like vacations, rewarding life journeys are based on careful and realistic planning, never on visions that exist only in the travelers' minds.

Chapter 6
The Trouble with Stepbrothers and Stepsisters

. ANGELA .

Angela hadn't seen her father in almost two years. He moved after the divorce and didn't call or write much after that until last spring when a letter from her father arrived inviting Angela to spend the summer with him.

The day the divorce was final, Angela's father had remarried—a woman with three kids. A new baby came about a year later, a girl. Angela's mother was still bitter. "A man who doesn't take care of the kid he's already got has no business bringing more into the world."

Angela wasn't sure what she thought about having a half sister. She liked babies and was kind of excited about it (though she never let her mother know). She was even more excited because she would have a stepsister her own age. She could hardly wait to get there. Angela and her sister would go places and do things together. They'd share secrets, fix each other's hair, shop, and trade clothes. It would be great! And there were twin brothers, too! Angela always had wished for a big family. Now she'd have one.

Angela also wanted to be with her father again. They never spent much time together before, but it would be different now. Absence does make the heart grow fonder, Angela had discovered. They'd appreciate each other more from now on. She'd help with the paperwork he always brought home from work; he'd help her with school assignments. They'd go to movies and the park, look after the baby together; they'd be a real father-daughter team. A real family.

They met her at the airport—her father, Inez (her stepmother), the twins and Little Cutie (that's what they called the baby). After a brief, "My! How you've grown!" her dad rushed off to collect the luggage while Angela and Inez tried to think of something to say to each other. The twins seemed not to have noticed Angela's arrival. They chased one another in and out of the rows of chairs, upsetting luggage here and there, drawing glares from people on every side. Angela tried to make friends with Little Cutie, commenting on the fountain of hair that grew from the top of her head. But the kid took her fingers out of her mouth only long enough to scream every time Angela touched her.

"She doesn't like strangers," Inez quipped. "Boys. Boys! Stop that and say hello to your new sister." The twins zoomed past Angela and almost knocked her over. "Boys will be boys," Inez shrugged.

Angela was shoved into the back seat of a cluttered, smelly station wagon along with the boys and her luggage. Oblivious to her, the twins bounced around like rubber balls while Little Cutie stood between Inez and Angela's father, sucking her fingers. The toddler glanced suspiciously back at Angela from time to time. Each time their eyes met she buried her face in her mom's shoulder and whimpered.

"Where's Marcia?" Angela said.

"Mac? Oh, she's out with her friends."

Mac? Angela considered it a strange name for a teenage

girl. It didn't occur to Angela then that she and her stepsister might not get along. She did suspect it a short time later, however, when she was shown to the room Angela and Mac would share.

It was a shambles. There were clothes, books, records, and even trash scattered all over the furniture and floor. Posters of guys in black leather, girls in sequins lined the walls, many of them torn or falling off. A cannabis decal was plastered to the dresser mirror so that Angela could see only slices of herself. A bulletin board was covered with school photos. Freaks. That's what most of the kids looked like to Angela. Was her stepsister a freak?

"Just push things aside and make yourself at home, Honey," her father said. "By the way, we're taking in a movie tonight. How about looking after Little Cutie and the boys for us?" And he was gone.

Angela was jangled awake the next morning by an alarm that screamed from the other side of the bed. "Oh, please," she groaned. Nothing happened. "Hey," Angela called again. "It's hard to sleep with that thing ringing." A bare arm appeared slapping at the clock, then a face, swollen and scowling.

"If you don't like it here, Angel-face, go back to your mother."

Later, reflecting on that exchange, Angela decided it was the most civil of all hers and Mac's conversations.

All that month, Inez stayed busy with her bridge clubs, shopping sprees and tupper-ware parties. (Angela got to babysit for all those, too.) Little Cutie continued to howl whenever her new sister came near especially if anyone else was around to hear. The boys ignored Angela entirely or picked on her. Once she asked to join their card game. "You know how?" one of them asked.

"No, but I could learn," she said.

"You cannot," the other retorted. "It's a boys' game."

Angela made several attempts to spend some time with her father. They were awkward when they tried to make conversation. And Inez was often there between them. If not her, it was the precious Little Cutie who filled her father's time and his lap. Angela was bored and lonely. Her dream of one big happy family had turned into a nightmare.

The worst of it was Marcia. Mac was an appropriate name, Angela decided. She was always out with her freaky friends or had half a dozen of them in her room. They were sloppy, smelly, and rude. They mostly ignored Angela or got very quiet and stared when she entered the room. Sometimes they snickered, too. Like Mac, they called her *the Angel* and made fun of her accent, her walk, and her clothes. She tried to avoid being around them.

But one afternoon they tramped into the bedroom where Angela was reading. While her friends sprawled over floor and bed, Mac switched the radio to a rock station and turned it up. Angela tried to concentrate on her reading, but it was a hot day and the music, the odors, and the laughter began to close in on her. "Hey, Mac," she said. "Does the radio have to be so loud?"

"What?" Mac's voice registered irritation.

"The volume," Angela called. "Could you change the volume?"

"Change the . . ." Mac hesitated then grinned devilishly at the others. "Sure, Angel," she yelled, spinning the volume control to maximum. "How's that?"

Angela's face grew red. She stood and pointed at the door. "How about playing your games somewhere else?"

"What'd you say, Angel? Can't hear a thing with the music."

"I was trying to read." Angela's nails dug into her palms.

Mac turned to her friends. "I can't hear a word the Angel

says, can you?" They shrugged innocently. Mac put a hand to her ear in a mock attempt to listen carefully. "What'd you say, now?"

"I said . . ." Angela grabbed Mac's hand and yelled in her ear. "I said, get out!"

"Wait a minute," Mac yanked her hand away and faced Angela. "If anybody's getting out, sister, it's you. This is my room, remember?"

The girls were suddenly shoving and screaming, scratching and pulling hair, kicking and crying. There were shouts and the crash of something breaking. Then the bedroom door flew open and Angela's father was suddenly there pulling the girls apart.

"What's going on here?" he said. "What's with you two?"

"I'll tell you what," Mac blurted out. "The Angel here marches in and turns her nose up at me and my friends. She tries to take over my room, fills up my drawers with frills till I can't even find my underwear. She uses up my make-up and stuff and then tells me to buy more. She even had the nerve to tell me I buy the wrong kind!"

"Look, Angela," her father sighed. "We never had this kind of trouble before you came. The other kids all get along. You're going to have to come down off your pedestal and be easier to live with. Otherwise I don't know what we're going to do."

Angela stood stunned. She saw a sea of faces surrounding her, condemning, despising faces, her father's as alien as the rest. "I'll tell you what you can do." Her voice was shaky. "You can take this . . . this pig you call a daughter. You can take your precious Little Cutie, your bratty boys, and your surburban housewife, and you can cram them." Angela's lip began to tremble. Tears welled in her eyes. "You treat her," she gestured toward Marcia, "more like a daughter than you do me!" Angela covered her face and sank to the floor sobbing. "I want to go home," she cried. "Please, just let me go home."

Whenever there is more than one child in a family, there are problems between the children. Cain and Abel are the classic example. Cinderella and her stepsisters are a folktale version. Angela and Marcia are a more recent one. Quarrels between brothers and sisters are so common that a phrase has been invented for the phenomenon—sibling rivalry. All families with children, including stepfamilies, see a good bit of sibling rivalry.

It's not hard to understand why brothers and sisters sometimes have trouble getting along. "Children fight for the same reasons adults do," Dr. Jacob Kirman, a psychologist, has said. "There are limited resources and each child wants more than he or she can get." The first child in a family enjoys the parents' total attention, he or she has them all to herself—until the second child comes along. Suddenly everything must be shared, not just treats, toys, and perhaps a room, but worst of all, Mother's time and love, Dad's praise and attention, Grandma's goodies, and Grandpa's knee. The older child resents being upstaged by the young intruder. The younger child feels bullied and pushed about. Each feels jealous of the other; each feels the other has a better deal; each fears the parents will love the other better. Every addition to the family complicates the situation more.

Since children from two or more families are brought together in the stepfamily, sibling rivalry is more intense than ever. Though some few stepbrothers and stepsisters adjust to their new relationships fairly easily, most stepsiblings fight like cats and dogs, at least for a time. They fight over parental favoritism. They fight for position—to see who's boss. They fight over everything, just like biological siblings do.

But biological brothers and sisters have some advantages

stepsiblings don't have. For one thing, they are able to adjust to one another slowly, while stepsiblings are thrown together suddenly and expected to act like a family instantly. Not only that, but when biological brothers and sisters do fight, they are carried over their squabbles by a sense of loyalty—loyalty to their parents, to their blood relationship, to the family. Subconsciously, brothers and sisters often feel as if they are extensions of one another. They feel part of one whole. Therefore, they know they must work out their differences. They know they belong.

Stepsiblings feel no kinship (in the beginning). They have no blood bond or sense of family loyalty to carry them over the rough spots. They don't yet feel as if they belong.

Biological siblings have another advantage. They have a shared and reassuring past. In growing up together they've learned that moments of rage and anger pass and that good feelings will again return. Stepsiblings do not have a shared past. Therefore, their feelings of resentment and anger are more threatening. Their moments of rage are more intense. And because neither feels the other belongs, they have fewer reasons for trying to get along.

WHY TRY TO GET ALONG?

Sibling rivalry (including stepsibling rivalry) is not all bad, however. The kind of competition that goes on between family members "fosters individuality and helps develop talents and competency," according to Dr. Harold Feldman of Cornell University. In learning to get along with your stepsiblings, you will learn how to get along better with all the other people you meet the rest of your life.

Recent studies show that kids who learn to adapt in a stepfamily can adapt to other new situations better than kids from traditional families. We're living in a time of great change. Those who survive the changes best will be those who are most adaptable. You and your stepsiblings can give one another the gift of adaptability.

There's a more immediate reason for getting along. Fighting is uncomfortable. It causes tension, anxiety, and stress. You cannot choose whether your stepsiblings will be part of your family. Because of your parent's remarriage, they undeniably are a part of your life. But you can choose to try to get along better and that will improve the quality of your life right now.

I know you can't do it all by yourself. Getting along takes two (or more). Show this chapter to your stepsiblings; show it to your parents. Talk about the ways suggested for learning to get along better. And practice them.

When Parents Intervene

Learning to tolerate one another is difficult at best. But it's even more complicated when parents get in the way. In all families, parents can either help or hinder their kids' relationships. In stepfamilies, they almost always make matters worse.

There are lots of reasons why this is true. For one thing, parents and stepparents feel they are failures when their kids fight. They are eager to have one big happy family. And they see every sign of fighting between the kids as a threat to that dream. A common warning is, "If you can't say something nice to each other, don't say anything at all." Parents who prevent their kids from venting their anger are volcano builders. Eventually the anger is going to explode.

Every parent feels defensive for his or her own child; it's much easier to see the faults of other kids than to see the faults of your own. So when fights between stepsiblings occur, a parent may jump in to defend his or her kid. When this happens, the stepchild feels ganged up on. But he or she may be afraid to express anger to the stepparent. Instead she'll probably treat her stepsiblings even worse later on. The parents may again intervene. And a vicious circle has begun.

In other situations, stepparents overreact in trying not to show favoritism. When fights occur, the parent sides against his or her own child. Feeling wounded, the kid is likely to take his anger out on his stepsibling. The parent may reappear and another vicious circle has begun. In stepfamilies, vicious circles lie in wait round every corner.

Parents who compare and point up differences between their kids also hinder the development of good relationships between them. "Why can't you make good grades like your sister?" is the kind of comment that causes a kid to feel more angry than eager to improve his grades. It will also make him resent his sister.

A certain amount of sibling rivalry is natural. In stepfamilies, as in all families, parents do their kids a favor by letting them work out their own problems—with a few exceptions; physical violence should never be tolerated, nor should any one child be constantly picked on by others or bullied to the extent that she withdraws or is unable to express her own feelings.

Kids who work out their own conflicts end up better friends as adults.

Ask your parents not to interfere when you and your stepsiblings argue. And remind them that brotherly or sisterly affection cannot be forced.

When Your Stepparent's Kids Come to Visit

What is it like for you when your stepsiblings come to your home? Chances are, it's tough. A parent and child want to be together; they choose to spend time together. But stepsiblings have no choice. They are thrown together whether they like it or not. Almost all people resent situations in which they have no choice.

Some stepsiblings are lucky; they like one another right away and look forward to spending time together. But most kids, after the honeymoon is over, find themselves resenting having to share the back seat of the car, the dining table, their bedroom, and their possessions. Most of all they resent having to share their parents, other siblings and friends.

Besides having to share everything that was once yours with stepsiblings, there may be other irritating things about their visits. One of them is this: A change may come over your stepparent before and during their stay. He or she may get all excited and bustle about planning, shopping, looking especially happy just before they arrive. And when they arrive, he or she will probably show them a lot of attention, play with them, take them places, laugh with them and have great fun. All these things may cause you to feel left out.

How would you (do you) act when this happens? There are three typical responses to feeling left out. See if one of them (or a combination) is your style.

1. *Some young people withdraw.*
They mope around, feel bad, shy away from all the excitement and noise while wishing they were a part of it all. People who act this way are even more likely to get overlooked and ignored in all the excitement. They may remain unhappy for long periods of time without anyone else ever becoming aware of their unhappiness. Silently, they just become more and more unhappy. So withdrawing is not a good way to deal with feeling left out.

2. *Instead of withdrawing, some people try their hardest to be number one.*
They try to outdo their stepsiblings—to be nicer, smarter, more talented, prettier, more likable. They desperately want to be better in their stepparent's eyes and heart than his or her own children. Unfortunately, this kind of com-

petition is like a carousel. It goes round and round but never arrives anywhere. And nobody wins. So competing with your stepsiblings is not a good way to deal with feeling left out either.

3. *The third kind of response to visits from stepsiblings is acting up.*
Some kids turn into living pogo sticks when the other kids arrive. They bounce around and twitch or wiggle. Because they're nervous, they talk too much and too loud. They show off or clown around to get attention. But instead of getting attention, what these boisterous kids usually get is in trouble. Their parents scold or punish them. The other kids complain, ignore or ostrasize them. So acting up is another bad way to deal with feeling left out.

Then what is a good way? What can you do when your stepparent's kids come around and you feel displaced?
There are several things that can help.

1. *Relax.*
The first step on the road to confidence in the face of visiting stepsiblings is to relax. That's right! Take a deep breath and relax. No actor ever performed well when all tensed up. Neither can you. Just remember that your stepsiblings' stay is only temporary; they'll be in your home only for a while. Remember, too, that your stepparent only sees the other kids occasionally while he or she lives with you. You'll get your share of attention at other times. You'll be more yourself and more likable if you can relax.

2. *The second thing you can do is forgive.*
Your stepparent misses his or her children and probably feels guilty about not living with them anymore. Your stepparent may also feel guilty about giving you time, atten-

tion, and money that no longer can be given to his or her own kids. When they do come, your stepparent may try to make up for all he or she feels they are missing by showing them a great time, ignoring their misbehavior, lavishing them with gifts and outings. Be patient if you can. This kind of behavior usually changes before long. Parents and kids too grow tired of amusement parks, movies, toy stores, and ice cream parlors. They eventually relax into a more normal pattern of family relating, one that will include you, too.

3. Ask directly for what you want and need.

Your stepparent may be unaware that you need more reassurance when his or her kids are around. And he or she will never know unless you speak up. Ask your stepparent to let you know you are cared for, too. Go to your stepparent for extra hugs and pats when the other kids are there. Most stepparents respond warmly to direct requests for attention and affection.

Some few stepparents, however, are not able to give outward signs of affection. Perhaps because of their feelings of guilt, perhaps for reasons no one, not even they, understand, these few people remain aloof and cold toward their stepchildren. If, after asking your stepparent for more consideration and more equal attention, he or she still does not give it, remember that it is not because of you or something you have done. It's because that person is simply not capable of giving freely.

WHEN YOU'RE THE VISITOR

What happens when you're the visitor with a parent who has stepchildren? "They always make me feel like I don't

STEPBROTHERS AND STEPSISTERS . 115

belong," one girl said, "like I'm in the way." A lot of kids feel this way. There are jokes they do not understand, games they don't know how to play (or are excluded from), and abilities they are made fun of for not having. It's often made quite clear that the house, yard, and belongings are *ours* not *yours*. And so are the friends. It almost seems as if there were a conspiracy to make the visitors go away and never come again. Sometimes that's just what happens.

But it need not be so. If you have encountered such a conspiracy, it may help to understand first why your stepsiblings shut you out. Secondly, it may help to know some of the things you can do to change the way things are.

Fear is one reason kids shut out new stepsiblings. Often brothers and sisters become very close when a divorce occurs. Through this turbulent transition time, they have a greater need to stick together and to support one another. They may even come to feel that they can count on one another and nothing else in this world. Their sibling bond becomes tighter; their distrust of others stronger.

This kind of closeness makes it even harder to accept a newcomer in the family. In fact the appearance of a stepparent and stepsiblings causes them to feel defensive. They cling to one another more tightly than ever and present a united front against the outside world. They are afraid of losing their own close relationship. So they try to maintain it by shutting out a new stepsibling.

One way to deal with this kind of solidarity is to take note of it, accept it, and wait for it to go away. If your behavior toward your stepsiblings continues to be friendly, they will grow to trust and accept you. They will learn that you are not out to get them and will quit trying to get you first. Eventually their fears will go away.

If your stepsiblings shut you out, it's probably because they're afraid of you, afraid you'll take some of their parent's love, afraid you'll take room, food, clothes, money, and other things that had belonged to just them. In part, they're right. When a family grows larger, they do have to spread their limited resources thinner (money, room, etc.). But there are also some advantages to having a larger family. Use all the patience you have in waiting for your stepsiblings to accept these advantages and you.

That doesn't mean, however, that you have to let them walk all over you. You can remind them, when necessary, that you are in your own parent's home just as they are. You belong in that home just as they do. Tell them to let you know if you're doing something that bothers them; perhaps you could do it differently. But if it's just your presence that bothers them, tell them they'll just have to get used to that. You are going to be around. Remind them, in a pleasant joking way when possible, that it takes more energy to frown or fight than to smile and get along. Tell them you'd like to get along. But it takes two.

One other way to deal with trouble is to talk with your parents about it. You wouldn't want to run to them over every little squabble. You'd soon be labeled a crybaby or tattletale. But you can and should tell them if you're being abused or constantly treated nastily. And you can ask for their support in establishing your right to be in their home. A good way to make your problem clear is to bring it up when the entire family is together, for instance at mealtime. Tell them that you're feeling like an outsider. Say that you'd like to feel more a part of the family, that you'd like to have a place for your things, to help with the chores, to participate in regular family activities. Tell them you'd like them and you to feel you belong.

Relating with stepbrothers and stepsisters isn't easy. But you and they can learn to receive one another politely and, perhaps, in time, with open arms.

When a New Baby Arrives

After remarriage, a new baby sometimes arrives. And a whole new set of complications arrives with it. Children from a former marriage feel excited and proud. At the same time they feel anxious, jealous, and resentful. More than anything else, they feel confused.

If you have a new baby in your family, it may help to know that it's natural to have both good and bad feelings about it. Most kids do experience a seesaw effect: jealousy and pride. The new baby takes up a lot of time, after all. Parents hold it a lot, feed it often, and change it regularly. All kids wonder, when a new baby comes along, whether their parents love the baby more. Not only that, grandparents, friends, even strangers pay more attention to the baby. People ooh and ahh more over an infant than over older kids. Sometimes it may seem the baby is getting everything and you're getting nothing.

These feelings come and go however. There are also times when it feels really good to have a little one around. When you help take care of the baby, you feel needed. When you get to show it off, you feel proud. You learn how helpless an infant is and gain priceless experience that comes in handy when you baby-sit and when you have children of your own. You also discover what it's like, as the child grows older, to be looked up to and admired by a younger sibling.

A new baby can be like a bridge in a stepfamily—it can connect the two sides together. Because the baby is related to everyone, everyone can feel involved in caring for him or her. The baby is a biological tie that can bind the entire family together.

All these positive feelings may pale, however, if the question of baby-sitting comes up again and again. Older kids in all families are needed to help with younger ones when a parent is busy or must run an errand. But kids who are required to baby-sit too frequently, every time their parents go somewhere, become understandably resentful. Unfortunately they take their resentment out on the person least able to help the situation—the baby.

Many families work out the baby-sitting this way. Older kids help out during brief intervals when a parent is busy or must run an errand. But when regular or lengthy baby-sitting is needed (for an afternoon or evening), the older kid is given the opportunity to baby-sit but isn't required to. If he or she is busy or does not want the job, another baby-sitter is engaged.

Talk with your parents about the kind of baby-sitting guidelines you'd like to see in your family.

WHEN YOU HAVE TO SHARE A ROOM, A TELEVISION, A FRIEND

There are certain things in all families that must be shared. Most siblings must share a room. And the sharing of a bedroom is often the root of many sibling squabbles. If you share a room, you and your roommate probably argue sometimes over who messes up the most, who has to do the most work in keeping it clean, who got into whose things, who gets to have a friend over next, and many other issues.

One way to avoid such conflicts is to ask your parents to help you arrange your shared room with a screen, a curtain, or another type of partition. Even the smallest room can usually be divided so that each of you has your own space to sleep in, to dress in, to study in, to keep clean or messy, to use as you wish. You can also make a habit of requesting permission before using any of your roommate's things. And ask him or her to be equally courteous to you. Sharing a room can be a bother at times. But it can also allow sisters or brothers to develop a closeness that they might not otherwise have developed. It's nice to have someone else around when you wake up from a bad dream. Sharing a room is not all bad.

There are other things—clothes, books, records, etc.—siblings can share with one another. Sharing allows each to have more than either would have alone. However, if arguments over clothing and other loaned items are to be avoided, some rules must be established and followed. You and your siblings can sit down together and work out the agreement that works best for you. You might begin with this rule: No one borrows another's things without asking first. Never. Another rule is that when borrowing an item, the borrower says when it will be returned, and then returns it by that time. A third guideline might be that an item must be returned in at least as good condition as it was when borrowed. If broken or ruined, it must be replaced. A final element of the agreement might be that, if any of the above rules (or whatever rules you agree upon) is broken, the borrower may lose the privilege of borrowing again for a specified amount of time. It should also be understood that no one has to loan anything he or she doesn't want to loan. Guidelines that are set out clearly and specifically (write them out if you wish) can prevent many an argument over property and allow you and your stepsiblings the privilege of sharing your things without the pain of fighting over them.

Friends are another matter. One of the most difficult things to share is a friend. Siblings have to be considerate of one another's rights to have friends, to bring them home, to talk with them on the phone, and to go places with them without interference. A tag-along, except when invited, is not usually appreciated. It's also best to avoid criticizing one another's friends and dates. It doesn't cost much to keep your opinions to yourself.

Some siblings run into the problem of dating one another's friends. In this case, it seems best to keep straight who the friend has come to visit and for each to allow the other time to be alone with that particular friend. Winning a friend away from a sibling for oneself is sure to bring on full-fledged war within the family. It is a violation of trust, of friendship, and of family ties.

If you have a sibling who makes butting in on your friendship a habit, ask him or her to read this chapter. Talk the situation over. Express your feelings openly—say you resent the intrusion. And ask him or her to allow you your friendships without intruding on them.

On the other hand, sisters and brothers sometimes need someone to hang around with. So you might consider inviting a stepbrother or stepsister along occasionally. Be sensitive to the loneliness and isolation that can result from the need for someone to be with. Sisters and brothers, stepsisters and stepbrothers, can be friends, too.

WATCH OUT FOR SAME AGE AND SEX

If you and a stepsibling are about the same age, or if you're the same sex, or both (like Angela and Marcia), watch out! Studies show that the closer siblings are in age, the stronger the competition between them. Also, siblings of the same sex generally have more conflicts than brother-sister pairs. This doesn't mean it's impossible for you (or for Angela and Marcia) to learn to get along. It just means that you may have to work a lot harder at it.

On the other hand, many stepsiblings who are close in age or of the same sex become great friends and are delighted to have someone with whom to share common interests and problems.

HOW STEPSIBLINGS CAN HELP YOU OUT

All the problems mentioned in this chapter may have made it seem that getting along with stepsiblings is impossible. It isn't. In fact some stepsiblings become great friends. And almost all stepsiblings eventually find that they have benefited in some way from one another.

How? For one thing, a stepsister or stepbrother usually has some abilities, talents, or knowledge that you don't have. They can be shared with you. You may learn new hobbies, new pastimes, new games, new job opportunities. My daughter learned from her stepsister how to play cards, something she has been delighted to be able to do with other friends.

Stepsiblings can also help you overcome the effects of family stereotyping. Often a family begins to label one child "the smart one" and another "the athlete." Or they may believe, because no one else in the family has ever been good with his or her hands, graceful on the dance floor, or a whiz at math, that you cannot be good at these things either. "The Joneses never could pass an English class" is a common kind of belief in families. The unfortunate thing about such belief systems is that they can trap you into believing things that don't have to be true.

You may indeed be a smart person. But that doesn't mean you cannot also be an athlete. A stepbrother who plays ball can teach you how. A stepsister who has learned make-up techniques, a variety of hair styles, and clever ways with fashions can help you learn to make yourself pretty, too, even if neither you nor anyone else has ever thought of you as pretty. You can learn about music, handicrafts, social skills, and many other things just from being around stepsiblings who excel at these abilities. And they can learn from you. Together you can break out of the old belief systems your families may have imposed on you.

Another of the benefits of having stepsiblings is that they can help you counter the effects of the birth-order factor. Let me explain what that means. Studies have shown that a person's character is strongly influenced by his or her chronological birth position in the family. For example, the oldest child in a family is more likely than the others to become a high-achiever—a manager, doctor, lawyer, or executive. Second-born children more often cultivate the social skills; they're usually popular with their peers. Children in the middle, on the other hand, often feel overlooked, while the youngest child feels alternately favored and deprived; he or she may receive more attention but also gets all the hand-me-downs. The youngest may also despair of ever catching up or of being treated as an equal. Each of the birth positions has its advantages and disadvantages.

When stepsiblings come into your life, it's likely they will change your birth order in the family. Instead of being the oldest, you may become a younger child or one of those in the middle. This change may be confusing at first. You might, for example, lose some of the privileges you had as the youngest. But the change can be helpful too. It can allow you to experience more than one role and, therefore, to have a more rounded character than you would have otherwise. If you were the oldest but are not now, then some of the responsibilities you were expected to fulfill may be shared by a new older sibling. If you were the youngest, and are no more, the tendency to refer to you as "the baby," will disappear. Whatever your position, having stepsiblings can allow you to experience more things, to learn more things, to become more of whatever it is you wish to be.

Stepsiblings can also help you to learn to cope with life. From the love and hate, fun and quarrels, ups and downs of brother/sister relationships, you can and will learn a lot about how to get along, how to bargain, how to cooperate, how to fight, how to accept differences, and how to love.

Parents and stepparents want their children to get along. They know that young people can give strength and support to one another. They can be advisers, listeners, friends. Stepsiblings can do all these things for one another.

They can also be a pain, as Angela and Marcia quickly discovered. But Angela and Marcia have time. They will have other opportunities to learn to get along. And the next time they meet, they and their parents will be more aware of the complications of stepsibling relationships. They will be better prepared to face those complications and to work through them. It won't be easy. But it will be worth it, because family members will have learned new respect for individual differences, better ways of coping, more life skills, greater flexibility.

Stepbrothers and stepsisters may be the greatest gift parents can give their kids. As one teen said, "I wouldn't trade my stepsister for anything. She's my best friend."

Not all stepsiblings can become best friends. But they can develop a relationship that works. They can become loyal to one another and to the future of the family. They can learn not to envy one another's abilities but to feel proud and fulfilled by the accomplishments of each.

Although stepbrothers and stepsisters have no blood bond to keep their relationship afloat, they can build a bridge of trust and respect that will weather any storm.

Chapter Seven
Discipline: What's Fair and What Isn't

. RUSTY .

Rusty peeled away from the light like a silver streak, leaving behind the smell of rubber. He'd had no idea when his father called this morning and picked him up that they were going shopping for a car. A car! But when Arnie, Rusty's dad, got an idea, he moved on it. And he got the idea to buy a car today, so Rusty was driving home in his own car today.

Home. When Rusty thought of returning home to his mom, little sister, and stepfather, his spirits took a dive. Rusty had been used to being the only man of the house; he came and went as he pleased, ate what he wanted when he wanted and lived like a man. Then his mother married Harold.

Harold expected Rusty to act like a baby again—at the age of sixteen! Every time Rusty started out of the house Harold wanted to know where he was going, what he'd be doing, who he'd be with and when he'd be home. And he was a maniac about money. He owned half the town, but trying to get a dime out of him was like trying to squeeze water out of a cactus. Rusty wondered what his mother saw in Harold; he was a hard man and unforgiving. But he knew his mother wanted only to be taken care of. Which was exactly what Rusty didn't want from Harold. All he wanted was to be left alone.

But Harold wouldn't do that. He badgered Rusty constantly to get better grades. If not that, then to get a haircut. And if Rusty got a haircut, then Harold hounded him to get off the phone, watch less TV, clean his room, sit up straight . . . the gripes went on and on. Rusty hated the hours from six in the evening until eight in the morning. Those were the hours Harold was home. And those were the hours Rusty did his best *not* to be at home.

That didn't work either. Their latest fight had resulted in Rusty's being grounded after school. Harold had also taken away his TV privileges (including the electronic games Arnie, his father, had given him). And he couldn't talk to his friends on the phone either. All over a little trouble he'd gotten into at school.

Harold's latest gripe was that Rusty didn't have a job. "It's time you started acting your age," he kept saying. "You got to take some responsibility for yourself. You got to get out there and hustle a little. Why, when I was your age . . ." That was Harold's favorite phrase. "Why, when I was your age . . ." It made Rusty's head ache.

Rusty swung into the drive and parked right beside Harold's dark green monster of a car. The Silver Streak, that's what Rusty would call his little jewel. He ran his hand along the dash and smiled. Moonlight glinted off its hood and put Harold's squat machine in the shade. Harold declared Rusty couldn't have a car until he worked and paid for it himself. Well, he thought, we'll just see what old Harold has to say now.

. *HAROLD* .

A self-made man. That's how Harold liked to think of himself. At the age of twelve he took a part-time job in a hardware store and kept the job through high school. He became assistant manager and worked on a couple more years after that. He had a goal. He pinched pennies, walked instead of buying a car, cut cardboard to fit in his shoes when the soles wore out, and had his mother trim his hair instead of going to the barber shop. The day he turned twenty-one, Harold opened his own hardware store. Within three years he'd moved his mother into a new house away from the railroad tracks. Within five years, he owned twelve stores in three different states. Harold understood hard work.

But he didn't understand his stepson, Rusty. The boy was going on sixteen and he hadn't yet kept a decent job. He'd worked at several. But he was often late to work (if he showed up at all), or he did a sloppy job, or he let his friends hang around and keep him from working. One way or another Rusty managed to lose every job Harold had helped him get. It was exasperating! Well, the kid was going to have to get out and find his own job this time. And Harold was going to see that he did so.

It wasn't the money he cared about; Harold made plenty of money to keep his family well. It was the principle. If Rusty was to become a dependable adult, capable of taking care of a family himself, then he had to learn responsibility. And Harold knew who had to teach it to him. Rusty's dad certainly wasn't going to do it. Arnie was a truckdriver. But instead of working regularly he drifted from job to job working at each place only until his pocktes were full. Some example for a son!

Betty, Rusty's mom, wasn't going to do it either. She babied him too much, and she cowered whenever Rusty turned his wrath on her. Rusty conned money out of her daily until Harold came around. A buck burned a hole in that boy's pocket. He'd pour every penny he could get his hands on down a crummy electronic game and ask for more. Well Rusty had to learn that money doesn't grow on trees even if he had to learn it the hard way.

Actually, he wasn't a bad kid. Rusty just had no sense of responsibility. None. His appearance showed that. So did his grade reports, the clutter in his room, and the kind of friends he chose, the hours he spent in front of the idiot box, and . . .

Well Harold was working on all that. He knew how to deal with kids. Rusty was grounded now for getting caught drinking beer on the school parking lot. He wouldn't do that again. And Harold took Rusty's TV privileges away after the last grade report, so his grades were sure to improve. Rusty just needed a firm hand, that's all. He had to learn that Harold meant what he said, that he (unlike Betty) would carry through with his threats—and his promises.

Harold also knew the value of positive reward. So he promised Rusty that he would take him shopping for a good used car *if* Rusty would just get and keep a job for one month. That's all Harold asked, one month. "Just prove you can be responsible for the monthly installments," he told Rusty, "and the prize is yours. I'll even make the down payment for you!" Harold was sure that would do the trick.

But that was three months ago. And Rusty hadn't even tried to find work. He claimed to want a car so badly; Harold couldn't understand it. Well, he certainly wasn't going to get a car until he lived up to his end of the bargain. No way.

More and more Harold realized he had a big job on his hands trying to turn that boy into a man. A big job, indeed.

Rusty strode up the front walk, yanked open the door, then remembered everyone would probably be in bed at this hour.

He pushed the door quietly closed behind him, then stepped into the living room to find his mom and Harold sitting on the sofa staring at him.

"Your grade report arrived in the mail today," Harold growled.

"Oh God," Rusty sighed. "Are we going through that all over again? I'm going to bed."

"Just a minute, young man," Harold caught Rusty's arm. "We're going to talk about this first," he shook a yellow slip in Rusty's face.

"What do you want from me?" Rusty yanked his arm free. "What's it to you if I pass or fail? It's none of your business."

"None of my business?" Harold puffed. "Everything that happens is my household is my business."

"Harold," Betty touched his arm, then her son's. "Rusty, please sit down. Let's just see if we can't work something out."

So they sat and went over all the same old stuff again—responsibility, self-reliance, privileges, jobs. "Why, when I was your age . . ." There it was again, Harold's favorite phrase.

"I don't have to take this crap anymore," he interrupted. "I can walk out that door and drive away anytime I want."

"What do you mean you can drive away?"

"I mean I'm going to get in *my car,* the one my Dad bought, and drive away from here just like I came." Rusty started for the door.

"There's a car out there?" his mother said.

Harold grabbed Rusty's arm. "Arnie bought you a car?" Heading for the door, Rusty dangled the keys in Harold's face.

"You can't keep it," Harold snatched the keys.

"It's mine," Rusty grabbed but missed, "you can't take it away."

"You know the rules. You can have a car when you've earned it." Harold put the keys in his pocket.

"You can't do that," Rusty yelled. "Dad gave it to me."

"Arnie gets all the credit, all the loyalty, all the fulfillment of being a parent. I get all the responsibility."

"Now, now," Rusty's mother tugged at Harold's sleeve. "Let's sit down and work this out. We can work this out."

"You drove the car home?" Harold asked.

"Naw, I led it home on a leash," Rusty snapped.

"Don't speak to me like that, son."

"I'm not your son," Rusty bristled.

The argument grew more and more heated. Harold fumed about Arnie's irresponsibility, Rusty's immaturity, and the impossibility of keeping the car.

Rusty countered by insisting he had rights, too, and that Harold had no right to take away what his own father had given him. Betty flitted about trying to soothe first this one then the other.

"Do you realize," Harold shouted. "As your guardian, I'd be held responsible for any damages you caused in that car?" He shook his head. "I knew Arnie was an idiot, but I didn't know he was insane."

"Harold!' Betty protested.

Rusty clenched his jaw and fists. "Don't talk about my father like that."

"It's crazy," Harold insisted. "Giving a two-thousand-pound weapon to an immature child is . . ."

"Give me the keys," Rusty shouted.

"No." Harold's face was red. He was breathing heavily through clenched teeth. "Go to your room, Rusty," he growled. The boy glared at his stepfather. "Please, Rusty," Harold begged. "Before I lose control. Please, go to your room."

A few weeks before, Harold and Rusty had fought, literally physically fought, fists and all. Harold felt remorseful afterward and went to a counselor. Rusty had to give him that; Harold admitted he was wrong. But Rusty also thought trying to get Harold to change would be like trying to change the shape of a rock by squeezing it.

"Please, Rusty?" Betty pleaded through her tears.

Rusty looked at her. His shoulders drooped in a giant sigh. He rushed from the room, down the hall and threw himself across his bed. Then Rusty reached over and flicked on his TV (the TV he wasn't supposed to be watching) and turned the volume up as loud as it would go.

Ask any adult whether he'd like to go back to being your age again. The answer will more than likely be a resounding "NO!" "Youth is beautiful" a friend of mine once said. "But it's so hard, I don't know how any of us ever escaped alive."

Adolescence is an exciting but difficult time. It is a time of great change, of metamorphosis from child to adult, of moving from parental control to self-control, of becoming a separate and independent individual. The young person has to strike out in new directions, try new behaviors, experiment with different roles. The parent has to learn when to be supportive, when to nudge ahead, when to stand back and allow experimentation, when to say yes and when to say absolutely no. It is a difficult time both for parents and for young people. And the difficulties inevitably show up in terms of discipline.

For stepfamilies, adolescence is an even more traumatic experience. During their struggle for independence, adolescents find it difficult enough to accept discipline from a lifetime parent they love and trust. It is much harder to accept discipline from a stepparent who may be an unwanted intruder in their lives. If you and your parents are having trouble over discipline, you're not alone. It happens in every family. Especially in stepfamilies.

Why do parents (including stepparents) and young people

inevitably find themselves in conflict? It's because they have different concerns and because they see things differently. Parents see themselves as protecting and guiding their children. Kids see their parents as restricting and controlling. Parents have a tendency to think in long-range terms. Kids concentrate on the here and now. Parents worry about health, safety, and pregnancy. Kids are willing to take a few risks in the name of fun, excitement, and experience. Parents want to know where their children are and what time they'll be home. Kids want the freedom to move about spontaneously and to do "what feels right." They don't want to interrupt an evening with friends to call home, or to say "I have to be home by ten." A young person wants parental approval, but even more than that wants the approval of peers. And he or she wants other things too. A young person wants his or her own set of beliefs, ideas, and ways of doing things. He or she wants to be a person. And the process of becoming a separate person includes a certain amount of rejecting parents and their values.

WHY DISCIPLINE?

Sometimes it seems as if life would be much simpler if parents would just back off and forget that there is such a thing as discipline. Rusty certainly thought so. But there are several reasons why that wouldn't work.

One, a family cannot function without guidelines. For example, if there were no limits about how much money could be spent each month, by which members of the family and for what items and activities, some members might spend wildly for unnecessary items. And there would soon be no money for food, clothes, and a house to live in. The family could not survive.

A less extreme example: If there were no general agreement in your home about when family members should sleep, when they should eat and when they should or should not have company in the house, the coming and going would be chaotic. None of you might ever be able to get any sleep because some of you would always be awake making noise. You might never get to eat some of the things you love to eat because no one would be preparing regular meals to share. In order for some semblance of order to be maintained, a certain number of rules, limits, and guidelines must be enforced. And it is parents who are mainly responsible for making and enforcing rules.

A second reason discipline is necessary is this: Though you are now a child protected and supported by your parents, you will soon be an adult who must be capable of supporting and protecting yourself. In order to do so, you must learn what society expects of you and the self-discipline to conform to at least some of those expectations. For example, you (like Rusty) cannot keep a job if you are not on the job site during the hours your boss expects you to be there. You'll be fired if you have not learned the self-discipline to meet your employer's expectations.

What happens when the red light at a busy intersection quits working? Some people blast through without stopping. Others sit and wait endlessly for fear of colliding with oncoming cars. Some do have collisions. Horns honk. People yell. Nobody gets where he or she is going on time.

People cannot live together in groups (families, cities, countries, etc.) without rules, cooperation, self-regulation. And it's parents who must teach these concepts to their children. It's parents who must discipline.

There's still another reason for discipline—children want it. Wait! Before you laugh, let me tell you a couple of true stories, one about a boy of seven, the other about a teenage girl.

We'll call the boy Tim. Tim's parents had not been getting along for quite some time. His father had moved out. His mother worked and was seldom home. Tim was what some psychologists call hyperactive. He was never still, always into something, mostly trouble. One evening when Tim's father came by to see his mother, Tim was sent out to play. What he did instead was throw rocks at passing cars. He yelled each time he threw. Some drivers yelled back, some honked and shook their fists. Tim kept looking over his shoulder at the house, but his parents never showed any signs of noticing. So he kept on throwing rocks. Finally, he broke a windshield. The driver stopped and got out. Tim went running into the house. He crawled behind the sofa his parents were sitting on. They agreed to pay for the windshield. But Tim could not be coaxed out even after the stranger had gone. He just kept sobbing and yelling over and over again, "Why didn't you stop me? Why did you let me do it? Why?"

Karen's is another story. Karen and her mother generally got along fairly well. Karen could usually talk her mother into letting her do pretty much whatever she wanted to do, or they'd at least compromise. But then she received an invitation to go skiing with a friend's family. Karen's mother flatly refused on the grounds that the friend's mom had a poor driving record. Karen begged, cajoled, screamed, and got angry. But her mother never gave in. A few days later, after visiting a friend in the hospital who was seriously injured in an accident, Karen thanked her mother for not allowing her to travel with an unreliable driver. Karen's friend was paralyzed.

The conclusions of these stories are very different. But they make the same point: Kids want discipline. Most children and young people, like Tim, test their parents' discipline from time to time. New stepparents are almost certain to be tested. Kids push to see just how much they can get away with, just how far they can go. Unconsciously, Tim was really testing to see just how tightly his parents' love could hold him. They failed. And Tim's anguish shows just how badly kids need and want discipline. Effective discipline is one way parents show their love. Sometimes you can recognize the love behind the discipline and sometimes not. Discipline can be a kind of caring. But discipline can also be a kind of tyranny. Rusty certainly thought so. He did not see love in Harold's discipline, only the attempt to control.

The big question then is not whether there should be discipline, but what kind? Where? When? And by whom?

Who Should Discipline?

The biggest dispute about discipline in the stepfamily is who should deliver it. Should a stepmother punish stepchildren who visit only on weekends? Should stepchildren be required to obey a stepfather with whom they live? Should a mother prevent a stepfather from spanking her children? Who should make the household rules? And whose responsibility is it to see that they are obeyed?

There are no easy answers. Even the experts disagree. Some say the stepparent should set rules from the beginning and make it clear that, in the new household, both partners have equal authority. Others argue that the stepparent should make friends with the children first and approach discipline gradually after trust has developed. Some stepparents, like Harold, come on strong, determined to set things right and to run the household efficiently and properly. Others play a passive role and are reluctant to get involved. Nearly all stepparents feel unsure as to just how they should discipline.

Whichever way your stepparent has attempted discipline, you probably haven't liked it. Many problems between stepparents and stepchildren arise because the child feels the stepparent is trying to take over a role in which he or she doesn't belong.

You may feel your stepparent has no right to tell you what to do or to punish misbehavior. Your stepparent may not be sure either. Is a stepparent a parent? A nonparent? An almost-parent? Should he or she have any say in setting household rules? It can be very helpful for you and your parents (all of them) to talk about these issues. Who should set rules in a home? The father? The mother? Some rules by each? Can some of them be agreed on democratically by all family members?

It will be helpful if you and your family discuss these issues together. See if you can come to some agreements as to who is in charge, when, and how.

Much of the resentment stepchildren have of their stepparents results from the feeling that the stepparent is attempting to replace the biological parent. That resentment can be relieved if both stepparent and stepchild openly acknowledge the fact that a parent cannot be replaced. No person can ever take the place of another; each is unique. A stepparent can, however, be an additional parent. And he or she does deserve the right to help set rules and limits and establish order within the household.

STEPMOTHERS HAVE IT HARDER

Stepmothers have an especially difficult time when it comes to discipline. Most women are acutely aware of society's expectations of them. Your stepmother may have entered the new family with the need to prove herself, to be the perfect parent with perfect kids. When your appearance is not neat or clean, she may worry that other people will notice and blame her. Some of them will. When you talk too loud, laugh at the wrong time, tell a dirty joke, or make bad grades, she may worry that other people will blame her. Some will. A stepmother knows society is watching her to see what kind of mother she will be. Your maternal grandparents and other relatives may be especially on the lookout for ineptitude or neglect. They and others are watching for signs of the wicked stepmother.

There are other conditions that also affect discipline and the stepmother/stepchild relationship. In many families, it is the woman who is with the children more and who must, therefore, do most of the disciplining. Just the fact that you must be with your stepmother more can cause the two of you to have more conflicts. There are also many men who play a passive role when it comes to childrearing. They leave the disciplining almost entirely up to the women. These customs make it very difficult for a stepmother and stepchild to develop a good relationship. The stepmother feels obligated to set the rules and enforce them. The stepchild feels resentful and rebellious because most of the interaction between them is negative. Both are victims of the family situation. Both end up feeling angry and abandoned.

If you and your stepmother are constantly in conflict over discipline, perhaps the two of you can talk with your father and ask that he take a more active role in setting and enforcing household rules. Perhaps you and your stepmother can also find some fun things to do together, movies, walks, tennis, whatever you both enjoy, so that not all your contacts are negative. Rough spots are easier to negotiate in any river if there's also some calm sailing along the way.

STEPFATHERS AND DISCIPLINE

Stepfathers and stepchildren also have their disagreements when it comes to discipline. Like Harold, many men believe they should be strong, constantly in control, and authoritarian. They think the man should clearly be the head of the household and that all other family members should bow to their commands. Some also think their values are the only valid values to hold and try to insist that their children adopt those same values.

Young people usually respond with a great deal of hostility to an authoritarian stepfather. They feel he has no right to make constant demands of them, to order them around, to force his will on them. Often, the harder the stepfather pushes, the more stubbornly the stepchild resists. Tension mounts within the household. Frequent explosions are the rule.

In many such cases, what the stepfather needs is reassurance. Authoritarian behavior often signals not only the need to feel in control but also a fear of losing control. A man may believe that if his children do not behave exactly as he commands, then he is ineffective as a father and as a person. He may also see the situation as a power struggle. Negotiation may seem a form of giving in or of losing the battle.

If your stepfather is authoritarian, you may be able to give him and yourself a gift. You may be able to reassure him that you want to get along, that you want to find a set of rules that you both can live with. If you show him that you are willing to give a little, he may be willing to meet you halfway. Eventually, you may be able to lead him to the realization that cooperation, not competition, is the key to smooth family relationships. And you may be able to help him become your friend.

The question of who's in charge? has no easy answer. Every stepfamily must respond in its own way. Some experts suggest that both parent and stepparent arrange to be home during the initial few weeks of remarriage. (Vacation time can be used this way.) During this period, the biological parent can take on the responsibility for discipline while the stepparent has a chance to make friends with and observe how the children are accustomed to being disciplined. After that, whichever parent is on the spot when an incident occurs is responsible for enforcement of rules.

If you and your stepparent already live together, you cannot use this recommendation. But there are some other things you can do. First and most importantly, you and your entire family can sit down and discuss the question of discipline. Perhaps you can agree upon certain household rules (it helps to write them out) and who is in charge of enforcing each. The more specific you can be in making your lists, the clearer each of you will be about what is expected of you and the more likely you will be to agree rather than disagree about what you can and cannot do and about who has the right to discipline.

STATIC AND INTERFERENCE

Have you ever been watching television or listening to radio when static suddenly replaced the picture or sound? The static may have been caused by a hair dryer or other appliance in your house. Or it may have been caused by something outside such as an airplane. Whatever caused it, I'm sure you were bothered by the static. It interfered with what you wanted to do.

Discipline in the stepfamily often suffers from interference too. Sometimes the interference comes from inside the household, sometimes from outside. Always, however, the result is unpleasant static.

How do people within the household interfere with discipline? A parent may jump into a dispute between stepparent and child. A brother may jump in between his sister and stepparent. A stepparent may interfere in a parent/child conflict. Or a young person may jump into a row between parent and stepparent.

Why do stepfamilies have more trouble with interference than traditional families? One reason is that their relationships are newer and more fragile. And because of their past experiences, they are more afraid to allow conflicts to run their natural course. One family has already come apart; might not this new family dissolve also? The trouble is, unless the various stepfamily members are allowed to work out their differences, static threatens the functioning of the entire family.

A remarried mother who hears her husband and child yelling at each other is not yet confident that they can work out their differences. Her tendency is to jump in and try to help resolve the conflict. What she may not know is that her interference may only make matters worse. If she takes the child's side, the stepfather feels shut out of the family. If she takes the stepfather's side, the child feels abandoned and ganged up on. Her interference causes static in the stepparent/stepchild relationship.

In most instances, conflicts between any two family members are resolved best when everyone else stays out of the way. There are a few exceptions to this rule: If one family member is being treated grossly unfairly or is abused, then, of course, it is appropriate for another to interfere.

People are not the only kind of interference, however. Stepfamily members do not have a shared past as traditional family members do. And the differences in their pasts can cause static when it comes to discipline. For example, you may have been used to having the freedom to come and go as you pleased before your parent remarried. Your stepparent may have been used to requiring children to report where they were going and when they would be home. Your past will cause you to expect one thing, while your stepparent's past will cause him or her to expect something else.

If your ideas and your stepparent's ideas about discipline are quite different, the two of you need to talk these over and find ways to compromise.

A third kind of interference you may have to deal with

comes from the fact that you have two homes, two sets of rules to live with, two sets of parents. It can be confusing to be allowed certain privileges in one home and not in the other. It is also a hassle when you get in trouble for something in one household, say a bad report card, and then have to go through the same hassle again in your other home. It is helpful if the two sets of parents get together and agree on certain guidelines. You can also remain flexible. "When in Rome, do as the Romans do" is an old expression you can live by. When in your father's home, follow the rules of that household. When in your mother's, follow hers. You might also ask your parents not to punish or reprimand you twice for the same infraction. Instead, they could agree on which of them would reward or punish you for grades and other common situations.

SHE TREATS HER KIDS BETTER THAN ME

A scruffy old cat once lived under the storage building in our backyard. It was wild, didn't trust people, and always took off like a bullet whenever one of us stepped outside. When it had a litter of kittens, however, it became a different kind of cat. Instead of running, it stood its ground when we approached. The hair on its back rose as it hissed and spat at us. When protecting her babies, that harmless old cat became a vicious animal.

Human parents are defensive about their young, too. Some scientists suggest we may have inherited an instinct which compels us to look after our own young above all else. It makes sense for nature to give us such an instinct; it would contribute to the survival of the species.

Survival in a stepfamily is somewhat more complicated, however. Not all the young have the same parents. And those natural instincts may get in the way.

Kids in all families complain that they and their siblings are not treated the same. But stepchildren are even more likely to feel they are treated unfairly. Sometimes they are. Most parents and stepparents try very hard not to play favorites among their young. They want to be fair. But wanting and doing are two different things. Dr. Benjamin Spock, a child specialist, once explained that parents, even in a traditional family, cannot treat two of their own children exactly alike. Every kid is different. And each one will have a different relationship with a parent from every other child.

All parents tend to be somewhat blind to the faults of their own children. Dear Danny is never really bad even though he's terrorizing the neighborhood. And Sweet Sue is such an angel even though she put a tack in her teacher's chair. Parents can see other kids' faults quite clearly, however. And that includes their stepchildren's. Part of the reason a parent is blind to his kid's faults is that he or she sees the child as an extension of self. Judging the child harshly would be judging oneself harshly. And it just isn't human nature to do that.

But there is another side to the story. Children are rather nearsighted about their parents, too. And it's a good thing. Parents make a lot of mistakes in raising their children. But nature seems to have built into kids a natural forgiveness of their parents' faults.

This is not so with their stepparents. A stepparent's every fault is noticed, resented, and sometimes pointed out by his or her stepchild. Every move a stepparent makes, especially when it comes to discipline, is often seen as unfair. Even when a stepparent is trying the very hardest not to show favoritism to his or her own child, the stepchild may feel that favoritism is being shown.

The fact is, natural tendencies work against the stepparent/stepchild relationship. So stepparents and stepchildren have to work harder at tolerating, accepting and forgiving one another than biological parents and their kids do.

You and your stepsiblings will almost certainly not be treated the same. People are all different and they relate differently with one another. If you expect always to be treated the same you will be disappointed. But it's only natural for you to want to be treated fairly. If you and your stepsibling do the very same thing (for example, you both come in an hour late for the second time in a row), you should be treated similarly. But those situations are very rare. Parents continually have to deal with different circumstances, and they continually have to try to figure out just what is "fair." Even when trying their hardest, parents and stepparents make mistakes.

Let your parent or stepparent know when you feel you are being treated unfairly. Tell him or her politely but directly what you consider unfair. He or she may be totally unaware that you are feeling that way. When made aware, most adults are sorry for having hurt a young person's feelings and will try to avoid doing so in the future.

CHILD ABUSE: WHEN DISCIPLINE GOES TOO FAR

Some parents believe in spanking. Some do not. They prefer to use other means of discipline such as sending children to their room or taking away certain privileges. Studies show that either method works well. Children who don't receive spankings but are disciplined in other ways are just as well behaved. And children from loving homes who receive reasonable spankings are not permanently damaged either physically or emotionally.

But some parents and stepparents carry spankings too far. When the child misbehaves, sometimes even when he or she doesn't, these parents take their angry feelings out on the child in violent ways.

People who mistreat or abuse their children are not crazy or mentally ill. Instead, they are people who are under too much stress. They haven't learned to vent their anger in healthy ways. And they often don't know of any other way to discipline than to use physical force. Most abusing parents were themselves abused as children.

One of the saddest things about child abuse is that abused children generally feel they deserve to be beaten. Because a parent lashes out at them when they have done something wrong, they feel the parent was justified in what he or she did. Not so. While parents are responsible for guiding and disciplining their children, the law now makes it clear that no child or young person ever deserves to be bruised, burned, or beaten, no matter what he or she has done. There are better ways to discipline.

Every child feels mistreated at times. A young person often cannot understand why he is being punished and feels the parent is unfair. Sometimes the child is right; parents aren't perfect.

But being treated unfairly is not being abused. A spanking is not a beating. Going to bed without your supper is not being starved. Having to stay in your room for the afternoon is not being locked away permanently from all human contact.

What, then, is child abuse? How can you tell if the spankings or other punishments you receive are normal or if you are being abused?

If you are being spanked so hard that marks are still left on your body the next day, you're being abused. If you are sore and it's painful to walk, sit, or move, then you are being mistreated.

Tell someone. Show your school nurse or teacher. Or tell

some other adult such as your minister, a grandparent, aunt or uncle, or other close adult friend.

Don't be ashamed to show what is happening to you. Nothing you could ever have done, no matter how bad it may seem to you or to a parent, is reason enough for child abuse. There are better ways to teach young people how to behave than to abuse them. Your parent needs to learn a better way.

Many parents who abuse their children realize they need help but don't know where to get it. One such woman started an organization to help parents and their children. It's called Parents Anonymous and there are chapters in many large cities of the United States. If your parent is interested, he or she can check the phone book in your city or write Parents Anonymous at 2810 Artesia Boulevard, Suite F, Redondo Beach, California 90278.

There are other parent groups that can help a parent learn to control anger. Churches often have information about such groups. Check the phone book for family counseling services or mental health organizations. There are suicide prevention/crisis intervention centers in most cities that can tell you what services are available in your area and that can advise you what to do. There is also a toll-free (that means you don't have to pay for the call) Child Abuse Hotline. Just dial 800-252-5400 for help and information. And there is a National Runaway Switchboard for teens who need help or want to contact relatives: 800-621-4000.

You have a right to freedom from abusive parental behavior. If you or a brother or sister is being abused, what should you do?

1. Talk with your other parent.
Tell the truth. Explain what is happening to you and ask for help. Most parents will step in and demand a change.

But some, out of fear, timidity or insensitivity, will not intervene. What then do you do?

2. Tell a neighbor, teacher, counselor, or minister and ask for their help.
If the first person you talk to is unsure what to do, then talk to another. Make them understand you and your parent must have help.

3. Whenever a parent or stepparent starts to hurt you, don't just stay there and take it.
Run to a neighbor's house or run into the street and scream. An adult is not likely to continue abusive behavior if he or she knows other people will find out.

4. Spend as much time elsewhere as possible.
If you need a place to go to get your troubles off your mind check to see if there is a Boys Club or Girls Club in your neighborhood. Check your phone directory or write to Boys Club Federation of America, 771 First Avenue, New York, New York 10017 or Girls Club of America, 205 Lexington Avenue, New York, New York 10016.

Remember this—just because a stepparent or parent is abusive does not mean he or she hates or even dislikes you. Nor does it mean that you are bad or that anything is wrong with you. It simply means that the adult has not learned constructive ways to deal with anger. He or she needs help. But what you need is protection. Tell someone you trust.

Take care of yourself. You deserve it.

How to Stay Out of Trouble

Millions of cars travel our city streets and highways every day. Yet there are relatively few accidents. That's because the drivers cooperate with one another within a planned traffic system—lights, signs, and safety rules. This system allows each driver the freedom to get where he or she wants to go, yet it provides a maximum amount of safety along the way. Because it is well planned, the traffic system works fairly smoothly.

Some families work fairly smoothly too. Some have a lot of collisions. They play discipline by ear, make up rules as they go, punish and reward inconsistently. When there is no clear pattern of cooperation, there are a great many more disagreements than in families where the rules are clear and the consequences of behavior dependable.

If you and your parents have frequent run-ins, then you need to sit down together and work out a better traffic system. It can be done this way:

1. Identify the major issues.
Sit down together (the entire family) and make a list of the things you most often fight about—curfew, bedtime, grades, appearance, chores, room neatness, television, car, telephone, money, smoking, drinking, drugs, etc. Don't discuss the issues yet or try to decide how to resolve them. Just continue brainstorming until you feel you have a complete list of touchy issues.

2. Write out the rules.
This may be the most difficult step of all. It's also the most important. Use your list of troublesome issues and, one by one, work out the rules of your household concerning each. Both you and your parents will have to compromise on some of the issues. On others, they may be unwilling to compromise. Even so, it's much easier to do what's expected of you when you're sure what is expected. Ask your parents to be specific about what they want you to do and when. Include what will happen when the rule is violated.

It may take several sessions for you and your parents to work out this part of your traffic system.

3. *Review and revise regularly.*
As kids grow and change, the rules they live by must also be changed. When you feel a rule is too restrictive, ask your parents to sit down with you and discuss the possibility of revising the rule. Many wars have been prevented through negotiation.

In addition to working out a traffic system with your family, there are also some things you, personally, can do to avoid getting in trouble.

1. *When in doubt, don't.*
This is an old expression that is wise advice. Situations will arise that are not covered by your household rules. If you wonder whether you might get into trouble for doing something, ask first. Don't push your luck hoping no one will notice. Parents almost always do.

2. *Choose the right time and place to ask.*
When parents are tired or very busy, they're likely to respond negatively to any request. Wait until your parent is in a good mood to make requests.

3. *Reason rather than rant and rail.*
Yelling at people almost never makes them change their minds. Reasoning with them sometimes does. Struggling to get your own way is a lot like getting caught on a fence. The harder you pull, the tighter you're held. But if you ease up a bit, move a little closer, you just might be set free.

4. *Express your anger in healthy ways.*
Anger is a natural response to any situation we perceive as threatening or unfair. Everyone feels anger sometimes. But

not everyone has learned to release his or her anger safely. When you get mad, how do you express your anger? Do you slam doors, throw things, yell at the person who made you mad, cry, seethe silently, growl at everyone and everything in your path?

Have you heard the story about the man whose boss chewed him out one day? He went home and yelled at his wife. She whacked their child, he kicked his dog, and the dog ran out and bit the mailman. What did the mailman do? He went home and yelled at his wife, of course.

People deal with their anger in many different ways. Some of the ways are healthy and some are not. Holding anger in can be especially harmful. It can result in actual physical problems such as ulcers, high blood pressure, and accident proneness. It can also cause emotional disturbances, sleeplessness, underachievement, or extreme withdrawal. Rather than holding it in, practice some of the healthy ways to release your anger.

First, tell the person you're mad at that you are angry and why. In this way, you can avoid dumping on the wrong person. Getting your anger out in the open also helps clear the air.

Secondly, tell someone you like and trust about your anger. Letting off steam often allows much of it to evaporate.

Finally, any form of physical exertion is an excellent anger releaser. For example, jump on a trampoline, pound clay, lie on your bed and kick, scream into a pillow, jog, walk or ride a bike, scrub the floor or mow the lawn, use a punching bag, drive nails, slam a foam or plastic toy against a wall, jump rope, throw everything out of your closet or drawers then rearrange them in an orderly way. Don't let your anger make you ill. Choose one of these or some other physical activity that allows you to work out your anger. And use it often.

Stepfamily members have to tread carefully when it comes to discipline. They must continually ask themselves whether they are being too sensitive or unfair. And they must work harder at understanding, accepting, and tolerating one another.

But there are some positive aspects of discipline in the stepfamily. Some stepparents are able to see their stepchild's behavior more objectively than the biological parent sees it. They point out ways the parent can be more helpful and the child more understanding. They can offer advice and support when a young person is in a difficult spot with another parent. Also, when people work out a problem together, they often end up feeling closer than before.

Discipline can tear a stepfamily apart. And it will if family members take sides, gang up, or refuse to cooperate.

Discipline can hold a stepfamily together. It can lend a sense of rightness and make each member feel secure. Like so many things in life, discipline is neither good nor bad, it's merely necessary. Like the traffic system, it works best when the rules are clear and when everyone cooperates.

Chapter Eight
Sexuality in the Stepfamily

. LAUREN .

Lauren couldn't sleep. But she didn't want to talk either. Usually she and Carol giggled until midnight when they spent the night together. Tonight, Lauren was too embarrassed. She would never forgive her mother and Roger for what they had done tonight. Lauren lay with her face to the wall and wondered whether Carol would ever spend the night with her again.

Lauren had liked Roger when he first came around. And he liked Lauren too. That first evening Roger came to their house the two of them visited until midnight while Lauren's mother fell asleep on the floor. They had so much in common, she and Roger. Both were science fiction buffs. Both loved cooking outside on the grill. And they both loved music—Lauren played the piano and Roger the guitar. In those early days, they made a ritual of playing and singing together every evening. That was before Roger and her mother were married.

What bothered Lauren most was that the two of them had started acting like a couple of lovebirds. They cooed and nuzzled each other constantly, even in public. Lauren avoided being seen with them. She spent more and more time in her bedroom and closed her door at night trying to shut out the noises from the next room. She went for long walks on Sunday afternoons when they locked her mother's bedroom door for what seemed like hours on end. Once Carol had called and asked if Lauren could go to a movie with her right away. Lauren knocked on their door. "Go away," Roger yelled. "But I need to ask a question," Lauren pleaded. "Not now, Lauren," her mother called. "Later." Lauren had to tell Carol she couldn't go. But she didn't tell her why. She was too embarrassed.

And now this. This was the first time she had asked Carol to spend the night since the wedding. After dinner the love-birds sat on the sofa rubbing noses. Lauren led Carol to the backyard where they listened to her radio and talked until dusk. But the mosquitoes got bad; Carol wanted to go in.

"Who's in the bathroom?" Carol asked as they passed by.

Lauren blushed. "I don't know," she said, closing her bed-room door. Still the laughter and splashing could be heard. There were obviously two voices—a man's and a woman's.

"That must be your mom and Roger," Carol said.

"Who cares?" Lauren pulled her nightshirt over her head. They crawled into bed. Lauren turned her face to the wall and pretended to be asleep.

I'll never invite a friend to spend the night again, Lauren was thinking. Why do they have to be so gross? And why doesn't Mom act like a mother! She lay for a long time wishing her friend hadn't spent the night in their house. Would Carol tell her parents? Would she tell the kids at school? Lauren wished none of it had happened and Roger had never come around. She wished her parents hadn't split. She wished she could go to sleep.

Listening to her friend's quiet breathing, Lauren wondered what it would be like to go to sleep and never wake again.

All families must deal with sexual issues. While still very young, for example, children question their parents about how babies are born. And as they grow, young peoples' bodies go through very obvious changes that are sexual in nature. Also, all family members—all people—have sexual thoughts and feelings about other people in their own homes. In some families, these things are talked about openly. In others, there is no discussion at all.

Like other families, stepfamilies too must deal with sexual issues. But there are certain problems concerning human sexuality that living in step seems to complicate. Lauren's situation is the result of one of those complications.

Lovey-Dovey Parents Are a Pain

One of the issues young people in stepfamilies speak of is discomfort with their parent's sexual behavior. Today's adolescents know the facts of life. But in first-married families, like Carol's, they are not often presented with direct evidence that Mommy and Daddy make love. In fact, when told how people "do it," most kids immediately reply, "Some people, maybe, but not my folks!" Young people in stepfamilies, on the other hand, are made much more aware of their parents' sexual natures. The parents touch one another a great deal. They kiss long and hug much. They may even shower together or close the bedroom door for long periods of time. In short, remarried parents make it very obvious that sexual intimacy is an important part of their lives.

Like Lauren, young people are sometimes very uncomfortable with this knowledge. Some are embarrassed, others resentful. Many kids feel shut out and very much alone when they see their parent and stepparent embracing. They may pout or go off alone and keep their feelings hidden. Some misbehave to regain parental attention. But most parents remain unaware of the discomfort they are causing.

If your parent and stepparent are very obvious in their sexuality, and if that bothers you, there are two things you can do. One of them is to tell them. If you let them know you are bothered, they will probably be glad to try not to be so obvious. Perhaps you and they can compromise and decide that certain expressions of affection, such as simple hugs and kisses, are okay. But that certain other obviously sexual expressions might be saved for private times and places.

The other thing you can do is wait. Your parents will become more used to each other in time and less showy with their affection. You will also begin to relax and be less upset by their behavior, because you will find that their affection for each other does not decrease their affection for you. You may even come to feel comforted by signs of caring between your parent and stepparent. They can help reassure you that your new family is a loving family. And that it will remain a firm and secure part of your life.

Parents Who Are Upset by Adolescence

A girl named Joyce was very proud that her monthly menstruation period had started—just as every girl should be proud. It is an official sign of maturity. One day Joyce asked her father to take her to the store for feminine supplies. It was her way of telling him she had become a woman. His response was to thunderously refuse. He seemed upset and embarrassed and Joyce was puzzled.

There are parents who relate well with their children so long as they are young. But they respond to their adolescent's budding maturity with coldness or disapproval. It can help a young person to know that such a parent does not usually mean to seem rejecting. But that there may be many complicated feelings bothering a parent. For example, a stepfather may be aware that his wife is jealous of his attentions to her daughter. He may worry about his wife's feelings and, therefore, be afraid to respond warmly to the girl's need for attention. In other cases, a father may feel some sexual attraction for his daughter and not realize it is normal to have these feelings. He may reject her attempts to win his approval as a way of rejecting his own feelings.

In Joyce's case, perhaps her father couldn't stand the thought that his little girl was growing up. Or he may have felt threatened by his own feelings when he looked at her and saw that she really was very grown up and very pretty. Whatever the case, Joyce suffered. Parents are seldom so open with their disapproval of their child's sexuality. Nevertheless, the message is often clear enough.

If your parent or stepparent ever responds coldly to your growing maturity, remember this: Developing into a sexually mature person is a natural process that deserves recognition. Some parents simply have not learned how to respond to their children's sexual development with warmth and approval. In such cases it is not the young person who is in error. It is the parent who needs help in learning to respond appropriately.

THE INCEST TABOO: WHAT IS IT?

In every society there are rules people live by without always being conscious of what those rules are. Don't appear in public in the nude is one of those unspoken rules in our society. Some few people break the rule. But most of us follow it without much thought. You might say nude appearances in our culture are forbidden or taboo.

Another of those rules our society lives by is this—don't marry or have a love affair with another member of your own

SEXUALITY IN THE STEPFAMILY · 155

family. Some people break this rule, too, however. And when they do, we call it incest. Incest is sexual relating or marriage between any family members except the parents. In most cultures, including our own, laws have been passed to enforce the incest taboo. Long ago, people believed incest could cause many kinds of disasters. And the laws and punishments once used were too severe. But we also know incest can cause jealousy, guilt, and other confusing passions that are destructive to family harmony.

Just the fact that laws have been written concerning incest shows that it must have occurred fairly often. It did. And it still does. It happens in all kinds of families, rich, poor, first married, remarried, black, white, Christian, Jewish, American, and all others. One person can easily find another in his or her family sexually attractive. Here's why.

An interest in sexuality is very natural. Neither is it unnatural to have sexual thoughts and feelings about members of your own family. In fact, it's quite common. Research shows that almost all people, both male and female, have such thoughts. Sometimes we deny or repress our sexual impulses so that we are unaware of them. They may then appear in dreams or other ways.

If you have had sexual thoughts or feelings about a family member, you are not evil or bad. You're just like everybody else. It's how we act on those thoughts or feelings that counts.

Laws concerning incest have varied from country to country and, in the United States, even from state to state. Relatives as distant as thirty-second cousins have been forbidden to marry. In ancient Egypt, however, marriages between brothers and sisters of the pharaoh's family were legal. Cleopatra married her brother. (He also happened to be her uncle so that after the wedding he was her husband, her uncle, and her brother!) Girls of one religious group in this country sometimes married their fathers or brothers until an 1892 Utah state law prohibited the practice. Many states now offer and require counseling for families instead of assessing punishment.

There is a lot of disagreement about the incest laws today. Many people believe the laws are outdated. There is no good reason, for example, to forbid marriages between relatives, such as distantly related cousins who do not live in the same household. There are very good reasons, however, to protect the rights of children. Young people can easily be persuaded to do things that may eventually be damaging to their healthy development. They can also be overwhelmed by an older, more powerful adult. Today's incest laws are intended to protect the young.

Laws can help protect. But they aren't helpful when it comes to understanding human sexuality. In fact, our society does not do a very good job of providing helpful sex education. Movies, television, and magazines exploit our interest in sex. But they seldom teach us much about feelings or what to do with them. We don't learn much about these feelings in school or church either. Yet all people have sexual thoughts and feelings, sometimes about members of their own families. But each family is left to work out its own way to deal with sexual feelings.

Families almost never talk about these kinds of feelings, however. There are at least two reasons. One is that the feelings often remain unconscious, below the surface of awareness. Another reason these feelings of attraction are not talked about is the incest taboo—most people think it is wrong to feel the way they do, so they keep their feelings a secret.

Neither reason for not talking is a good one. For one thing, it's silly to feel guilty for feelings. Feelings—anger, sadness, desire, etc.—are neither good nor bad. They simply are. It makes as much sense to feel guilty for having sexual feelings as it does to feel guilty for having an elbow.

For another thing, it's best not to stay unconscious of our feelings. Instead, it's best if we talk about them and come to understand them, because if we accept and understand our feelings, we have a better chance of dealing with them in healthy, useful ways.

BROTHERS AND SISTERS IN LOVE

AN ESKIMO LEGEND

The sun and the moon that float over our heads once were brother and sister. And they lived upon the earth. One night, in a house where there was no light, they lay down together. And they loved.

But in the morning, when the sister discovered that her lover was her brother, she cried out in shame. And in her anguish over what they had done, she ripped off her breasts and flung them in her brother's face.

Taking a torch, the sister fled. Her brother followed with yet another torch. As the sister disappeared from view she rose into the sky. Her torch burned more and more brightly. At last, she became the sun. As he followed, the brother's torch spluttered dimly. He, too, rose into the sky. The brother became the moon.

Like the sun and the moon in this Eskimo legend, sisters and brothers often find one another sexually interesting. Very young children have a natural curiosity about their bodies. Brothers and sisters satisfy that curiosity by dressing and bathing together. Or they may play games such as "doctor," "I'll be the daddy, you be the mommy," or "Show me yours and I'll show you mine." It's all a very natural way for them to learn the differences between male and female bodies. Soon, however, most parents make it quite clear that they don't approve of such behavior.

Children's bodies blossom into adult bodies during adolescence. A renewed interest in sexuality also blossoms during this time. Siblings may again find one another sexually interesting. But those who have grown up together usually remain unconscious of these feelings. Because of the incest taboo, most brothers and sisters look outside the home for a girl-friend or boyfriend.

But what happens when young people who were formerly unrelated suddenly find themselves living together in the same house? They may be called brother and sister. But they probably don't feel that way at all. Stepsiblings can become such good friends that they drift toward becoming sweet-hearts. Too soon, they may be lovers.

In our society, intimate relationships between members of the same household are considered inappropriate. Stepsiblings know this. And because they know other family members and friends would disapprove, they end up feeling guilty. The necessity to play the role of brother and sister on some occasions and of lovers on others is confusing. Fears of being found out keep them nervous and upset. And jealousies arise concerning other friends, other family members, and other activities. Eventually the entire family suffers as a result of tension within the household.

For all these reasons, stepsiblings, like biological brothers and sisters, are better off if they do not act upon their feelings of attraction for one another. Sometimes, however, when the feelings are very strong, it is difficult not to do so. If you find yourself in this situation, you may wish to turn to a parent, minister, counselor, or close friend for help. There are also very clear guidelines at the end of this chapter that may help you to understand and deal with your feelings better.

FATHERS AND DAUGHTERS—MOTHERS AND SONS

Early in this century there was a doctor in Austria who believed all girls dream of marrying their fathers, and all boys long to take their father's place (though their dreams are not always on a conscious level). The doctor's name was Sigmund Freud. One name Freud gave to the feelings of attraction between a parent and child was the Oedipus complex. The following story will help explain why.

AN ANCIENT GREEK MYTH

There was once a King Laius and a Queen Jocasta who had an infant son. Their joy over the baby's birth was short-lived, however. For it was soon foretold that the child would someday kill his father and sit upon the throne.

With a heavy heart, King Laius ordered the child slain. The king's servant carried the baby into the forest. But he could not bring himself to kill the infant. So he left the baby pinned by his feet deep in the woods.

A hunter found the boy, took him home, and adopted him. The child was called Oedipus (swollen feet).

When he was a young man, Oedipus set out on a journey. By chance he and King Laius met on a narrow road. Neither recognized the other. And in an argument over who might pass first, Oedipus killed his father.

Sometime later, Oedipus was able to free the people of his father's kingdom from an evil curse, something no one else had been able to do. He became their hero, and they crowned him king. King Oedipus then married Queen Jocasta, not knowing she was his mother. They loved each other and had children together. But the kingdom was beset by disaster, blight, and plague.

At last, the king and queen discovered their kinship and despaired. Oedipus was sure that, because he had murdered his father and married his mother, he had caused all his country's troubles. Feeling guilty and depressed, King Oedipus gouged out his eyes.

Freud believed all of us are a little like Oedipus who loved his mother—we feel some attraction toward our parents. Not all of Freud's theories are considered accurate today. But we still speak of the Oedipus complex. That's because we know that parents and children often do find one another attractive. It's quite common for them to do so. And absolutely normal.

One father's dream explains very clearly the situation a parent and child find themselves in. The dream came one night after the father and his teenage daughter, Julie, had been to a church social. Julie asked her father to introduce her to a nice-looking young man. He did. "Then as I stood back and watched them," he said, "I became aware that she really is growing up, and that she's a very attractive young lady." Here is what he dreamed.

> Julie and I were walking along together, holding hands. Suddenly we were climbing a steep mountain. Still we talked and laughed. But as we neared the top, Julie grew solemn. She said that she was feeling things a daughter shouldn't feel for her father. I held on tightly and told Julie that it was natural to have those feelings. But she kept teetering near the edge of a cliff. I caught her again and again so that she wouldn't fall off. And I had to be very careful not to fall with her.

Was the father saving his daughter from the young man? From her own feelings about her father? From the father's feelings about her? From all these things? The dream symbolically represents the role every parent or stepparent must play with an adolescent. A young person continually needs friendship, warmth, and affection. At the same time, he or she needs an adult who will firmly maintain the balance of the protective, parent/child relationship.

In most families, that's how it works. But in some families, the people become confused about their roles. A father or stepfather who is himself in need of more attention and affection than he receives may attempt to fill those needs through a close relationship with his daughter. A lonely mother may try to fill her needs for warmth and love through a relationship with her son.

It may seem to you that this sort of thing could never happen. You may believe that a parent and child or young person could never really become sexually intimate with each other. But it does happen. And quite often. Thousands of cases are reported each year. And authorities agree that there are a great many more unreported cases.

How does it happen? How do a parent and child end up relating as lovers? In most cases, it doesn't happen suddenly. Instead, it is a gradual process, almost accidental. It may begin with innocent flirtations, the kind that occur in all families. The parent and young person may be affectionate with one another and sometimes play body contact games like wrestling and tickling. When other family members are away, they may caress and touch while watching television. They find one another's company comforting. Eventually they touch in more and more sexual ways. And finally their relationship has drifted far outside the traditional parent/child boundaries.

This kind of incident can happen between a father and his daughter or stepdaughter, or between a mother and her son or stepson. Or it may happen between a mother and a daughter or a father and son. These people are not evil-eyed ogres. Often, they are regular churchgoers, responsible citizens, and class leaders. The desires and needs they feel are normal. But the means they use to fill those needs are inappropriate.

Girls need attention from their fathers (or some other man who is important in their lives). Boys need attention from their mothers (or other important women). It is from relating with an important adult of the opposite sex that we learn to relate appropriately with other members of the opposite sex.

For example, if a girl is secure in her relationship with her father, she is much more likely to have a good relationship with her husband later on. If a boy and his mother get along well, he is much more likely to relate well with girlfriends and, later on, with his wife. (In single-parent and remarried families, a stepparent, grandparent, aunt or uncle, or other family member or close friend often fills this need.)

Girls try out their femininity on their fathers or stepfathers or other important men in their lives. "What do you think of my new dress, Dad?" a girl might say. Or, "Look at my new hairdo!" Boys practice their romantic inclinations on their mothers or stepmothers or other important women. "Look what I brought home for you," a young man might announce. Or, "Look, Ma. No hands!" What young people are asking for, at such times, is warmth and affection. They need approval for the changes in their minds and bodies. Most of all, they need an adult who is able to give approval and love but, at the same time, firmly maintain the role of parent or older friend.

Almost all family members flirt. It's one way kids can ask for attention and approval. And it's one way parents can give it. Flirting can be fun. But it can be dangerous, too. And it, therefore, needs to be done with care and with awareness of all that it may imply.

Flirting often has a serious message hidden beneath the surface. For example, a girl may flirt with her father or stepfather as a way of testing him. Or she may be trying out her own emerging womanliness on the safest male around. What she needs at these times is for him to respond with fatherly approval. She needs reassurance that she is appealing and will be able to attract a mate. A warm response helps build her self-esteem. But if what she gets is a willing romantic partner, she becomes confused. She may feel very bad about herself. And her emotional development is hindered instead of helped.

A boy may flirt with his mother or stepmother in the same way. He may bring her gifts or write poetry or songs. And he may tell her she is the object of his dreams. The young man may believe it would be exciting and wonderful to become her lover. But if she allows this to happen, he will almost certainly come to despise her for betraying both him and his father.

If you ever find yourself flirting in these ways, consider asking more directly for approval. Examine just what it is you want from your parent, and what you don't want. Then ask yourself whether your flirting behavior makes that distinction clear.

What's Wrong with Incest?

Everyone has sexual thoughts and feelings, sometimes about family members. If these feelings are so natural, some people ask, what's wrong with sexual loving between family members?

The loving, itself, may or may not be wrong, depending on your own personal belief system. But regardless of your beliefs, the consequences can be unpleasant and, in some cases, even devastating. For one thing, sexual relating between family members affects more than just those who are directly involved. It affects the entire family. Competition and jealousies are aroused. The parents' relationship often suffers. The other children become aware that one of them is being treated differently. And the young person who is involved may feel singled out and privileged or damned. The family's continued existence may, in fact, be threatened.

Perhaps the most destructive of all the possible consequences of incest is guilt. Most young people who become sexually involved with a family member end up feeling bad about themselves. They feel responsible for what has happened. Girls, especially, often feel they are defiled, nasty, or ruined. They think they can never again be good or be loved by a wholesome young man. Some feel bad about themselves and suffer all the rest of their lives.

These young people are punishing themselves undeservedly. No one person is ever entirely to blame when a sexual relationship develops between a parent and child—certainly not the young person. And he or she is only partly responsible when such a relationship occurs between siblings. A family is a cooperative venture; nothing ever happens in a family that does not involve every single member. All must share responsibility for whatever occurs. And it is the parents who must carry the heaviest share of responsibility.

All humans behave, at times, in ways that they are sorry for later on. Behavior is just that—behavior. And it is not a permanent part of us. We can change our behavior. We can act differently tomorrow than we acted yesterday. We can move beyond the past into a brighter future.

But sometimes we need help. Often families need counseling when sexual intimacy has occurred. If a parent has been involved, he or she must learn different ways to fulfill needs other than turning to a young person or child. When a young person has been involved, he or she often needs reassurance and help in overcoming guilt. Counseling can help. Talk to your minister, or look in the phone book for family or community counseling centers. There are also some specific guidelines at the end of this chapter; they can be helpful in maintaining healthy family relationships.

WHAT IF YOU ARE ALREADY INVOLVED?

If you and a member of your family find one another attractive, be glad you like each other and be proud of one another's attractiveness. But do not involve yourselves in sexual intimacy.

If you already are involved sexually with a family member, have him or her read this chapter and discuss what goes on between you. Relationships in families are generally too complex for sexual activity between any members (except the parents) to work out well. Life will be simpler and family relationships better if you put an end to the intimacy now. Consult a counselor if you need further advice.

Don't go about feeling guilty, however. Whatever you have done is in the past. It's what you do from here on that counts. Your past behavior need not in any way harm your ability to develop close, warm, and sexually satisfying relationships in the future when you're ready for them. Don't feel bad about yourself (or let anyone else make you feel bad). Think of the relationship with your family member simply as a way in which you learned more about yourself, about life, and about human sexuality. And use that knowledge well in the future.

Sexual Abuse

A parent is supposed to take care of and protect his or her child. So is a stepparent. Most of them do a pretty good job. There are some adults, however, who never learn to do this very well. Some abuse their children either physically or emotionally. And there are also parents who abuse their children sexually. Many of these adults were, themselves, abused as children.

There are two kinds of adults who become involved in sexual abuse of children or young people. The first is the parent, stepparent, grandparent, other relative or friend who knows and cares about the child. But this type of adult mistakenly turns to a youngster for sex in an attempt to fill his or her own needs for closeness and warmth. He or she is likely to persuade or coax the young person to cooperate. The child or adolescent may understand the adult's need and may be willing to try to help fill that need. Eventually, however, the younger person will feel betrayed.

The other type of abuser is much more harsh. Unfortunately, there are some people who simply have no appreciation or understanding of love. This kind of person is hostile, aggressive, and frequently a tyrant in the home. He or she may threaten the child with further abuse or with death should the child tell. And the threats of violence are sometimes carried out.

Both of these types of people need help. But it is the young person who is in the greatest need of help. Too often, a child is ashamed or afraid to tell what has happened. It should be told. And the adult should receive counseling or punishment depending on what has occurred.

In some families another adult is aware of what is happening to the youngster but does not interfere. In some cases, kids have told other relatives but were not believed. In others, they have been accused of causing the abuse themselves. Whatever the circumstances, the young person is not to blame. He or she is a victim. And there are adults who can help put an end to the abuse.

What happens to a parent when a child tells? In many states the entire family is required to seek counseling. Sexual abuse is often a symptom of other problems within the family, such as trouble between the father and the mother. In some cases the child is removed from the home to prevent continued abuse. He or she may live with other relatives or with another family until it is again safe to live at home.

If you are ever encouraged or forced to relate in sexual ways with a parent or other adult, take care of yourself by telling someone you trust about it. Tell another parent. If he or she does not believe you or will not help, tell another adult relative. Or tell a counselor, minister, teacher, or adult friend. Or look for the name of your state in the phone directory, then find the department of public welfare or the department of human resources. Under that heading you will see the children's protective services (young people are considered children until they are twenty-one in most states) or an information number. Call the number and ask for a social worker who could talk to you about problems at home. Keep talking to people until you find someone who will help. No young person ever deserves to be sexually misused.

Some young people feel guilty for what has happened. They feel bad about themselves. And they believe they are to blame. They're not. Nothing a young person could ever do or say is cause enough for betrayal. Adults are supposed to be more mature than young people. They are supposed to know that it is never okay to ask for or demand sexual favors from a child. To do so is a gross violation of trust.

Your Body Belongs to You

There was a time when a child was considered the property of the parents. It was believed that a parent could do whatever he or she wished with the child. That time is no more. Today there are laws protecting children's rights, including the right to grow up free of the problems caused by sexual misuse or abuse.

The topic of children's rights is popular today. Kids have more rights and protection under the law than ever before. Some people are now arguing that kids should also have the right to participate in sexual activity if they want. Those who oppose this view argue that such an attitude would permit more child abuse. What do you think?

Above all else, remember this: Your body belongs to you. Not to anyone else. You have the right to set limits on how it will be treated. You are not obligated to be nice to anyone, not even a family member, by allowing any kind of touching with which you are uncomfortable.

It's okay to say no. And it's okay to turn to someone else for help if that no is ignored or overruled.

You're a person, too. You have feelings, needs, and rights. You have the right to a healthy emotional development free of sexual harassment or misuse. Take care of yourself by asking for help if you need it. You deserve to be treated with respect and love.

GUIDELINES FOR HEALTHY SEXUAL ATTITUDES IN STEPFAMILIES

There are some important things about the guidelines in this section you should know. First, they are not intended to give the impression that human sexuality or the human body is bad or evil. It isn't. Sexuality is an important part of our lives. It is hoped that these guidelines can help you and your family understand one another better. And that they may help you to be proud of your sexuality and give it the respect it deserves.

There is something else you should know before reading the guidelines. One of the most important things Sigmund Freud discovered was that we should not try to ignore our sexual urges or push them away. In fact, if we try to repress them or deny their existence we can cause ourselves all kinds of adjustment problems. Rather than ignoring the sexual aspect of our beings, we can learn to accept, appreciate, and enjoy it.

Don't be afraid of thinking about your sexuality and of other people's. When you wonder about something, ask questions of a family member. It's best if families can talk about such matters openly. But if that is not possible in your family, talk with other adults you trust and respect.

Finally, remember this. Having sexual feelings, even toward a family member, is part of being human. It is not something you should feel bad about. Feelings and actions are two different things. You needn't feel guilty for whatever feelings you may have. How you choose to act on those feelings is what counts. Feeling angry at a family member is okay. Hitting is not. Feeling sexual interest in a family member is okay. But acting on those feelings is not.

Show this chapter to your parents. Talk about the following guidelines and decide which might be helpful in your family.

1. Bathrobes are appropriate when street clothes are not being worn.
Family members running about the house nude, or almost nude, may prove too stimulating for some young people and some adults.

2. Respect one another's rights to privacy.
Assign or allow for separate bathroom times. And knock before entering a bedroom or bathroom.

3. Parents of adolescent stepsiblings should avoid leaving them home alone together for long periods of time.

4. Establish who can go into whose rooms and at what times.
Rather than assigning stepsiblings bedrooms side by side, it might help to have them on opposite sides of the house. In some cases, it has worked best for one young person to live in his or her other parent's home for a while.

5. A parent and child should not sleep together on a regular, continuing basis.

6. Some experts advise a stepparent and adolescent stepchild of the opposite sex not to stay home alone together for long periods of time (a weekend, for example), not because they are likely to become intimate, but because they might feel sexually attracted and then feel guilty for their feelings.

7. Be aware that some body-contact games can heighten sexual arousal, especially if the games are too intense or go on for too long.

8. It is normal for an adolescent to seek attention and approval from the parent or stepparent of the opposite sex.

Sometimes these bids for attention take on the nature of flirting. At those times, it is important for the parent figure to respond with warmth and approval. But it is also sometimes necessary to remind the young person that the parent is not available as a romantic or sexual partner.

9. Talking about sexuality in the family is important.

For example, a mother may need open reassurance from her husband that he would never step outside the role of parent or friend with her teenage daughter. A father may need to be reminded that his daughter or stepdaughter continues to need affection even though she is beginning to look like a woman. Stepsiblings may need to be encouraged to talk openly of their sexual feelings for one another. They will then be able to understand them and to make responsible decisions as to how to act upon those feelings.

10. Affection, touching, and holding are important aspects of family relating.

Young people and adults need affectionate touching. But french kissing and thigh, breast, or genital fondling are the kinds of contact that go beyond appropriate limits. Just remember that your body belongs to you. You alone have the right to decide how it will be treated. And you have the right to say no.

11. Counseling often helps families deal with sexual issues in healthy ways.

Talk with your minister or a school counselor, or call a family counseling center.

12. Important! Don't let the other guidelines listed here cause you to feel uncomfortable with another family member.

For example, don't go about worrying every time your parent, stepparent or stepsibling looks at you, that he or she is thinking about your body. It simply isn't true. Sexual thoughts and feelings are fleeting things. And very natural at that.

People, especially children and adolescents, need hugs, kisses and caresses. Their feelings of self-worth depend, in part, on how much affection they receive. In order to be just plain healthy, in fact, people must have love expressed through human touching.

So express affection for family members when you feel like it. And allow it to be expressed in return. Link your arms together. Crowd up on the sofa while watching television. Hold hands. Massage temples or tired feet. Place an arm around shoulders or waist. Snuggle in front of a fire together. Families are at their best when secure in the closeness of human touching.

Chapter Nine
Stepping in Style

. GERRI .

I never thought I'd survive. I was fifteen when Mom and Bob got together. I'll never forget the day he arrived on the doorstep, arms loaded down, and announced he was moving in. Bob ordered me to carry boxes of his junk in from the car. "Carry your own crap," I said, and turned to walk away. He grabbed my arm, yanked me around and lectured me with his finger in my face. He said something about how he was going to be my father, and how I was to give him the respect a father is due. I blew up and said really awful things like, "Sleeping with my mother doesn't make you my father." Mom slapped my face. Bob literally dragged me to my room, slammed the door, and yelled that I would stay there until I could behave like a civilized human being. I yelled obscenities back at him. But secretly I smiled because I got just what I wanted; I got out of having to carry in Bob's junk for him.

That was only the beginning, however. Hate at first sight; that's how I described our relationship to my friends. Bob insisted I had to obey him. I soon learned not to say much, but with my actions I made it very clear that I would not obey. Finally one night I came in very late. He was waiting up for me and a noisy battle began. He cursed and I cursed. He slapped me and I spit on him. My mother was crying the

172

whole time and begging us to stop. Finally he beat me up (but not without his share of bruises and scratches) and locked me in my room.

The next day I hitch-hiked to my father's house. He was surprised and glad to see me. But I could see the gladness turn to worry right away. I told him and his wife all that had happened. He immediately called my Mom and told her I'd be staying with him. Bob made a point of not being at home when we went to move my things over the weekend.

I thought everything at Dad's house would be wonderful. I'd liked his wife before, but I began not to like her as time went on. She was gooey sweet when Dad was around but cold as a fish when he wasn't. I also hated how she acted like a baby when she didn't get her way. She was jealous of me and tried to keep me and my father apart. Finally, we had a big fight one night. She told Dad he had to choose; it was either her or me. Dad took her in the bedroom and they were in there a long time. Then he came to my room and had a talk with me. He said he loved his wife and didn't want to lose her, but that he'd always love me, too, no matter what happened. I knew what he was trying to say—that I'd have to move out. I felt all sick inside and couldn't say a thing. That night I took some pills I found in their medicine cabinet. When I woke up in the hospital, it was Bob and Mom who were there. They took me home with them, and that's where I stayed.

Bob and I were calmer after that. It was still clear that we didn't like living together. But we both accepted the fact that that's how it was going to be. At least I learned not to push his buttons, and he learned not to lean so hard on me. We still had plenty of fights, but he never threatened to throw me out again. And I never pushed him quite so far. When I look back on it all now, I realize Bob really did a lot for me. He paid for my clothes, my food, my braces, my education. He tried to be a real father to me. That was so important to him, to be a real father. But I didn't want that.

At Christmastime I always go back there—to Mom's and Bob's house. And it always feels good. We play golf together, Bob and I, laugh and have a good time. And we do our Christmas shopping together. I can see that Mom is happier than she's ever been. So I'm really glad, now, that she married Bob. But I'd have laughed in the face of anyone who told me back then I'd say that some day.

If I had to give advice to other stepkids, I'd say two things: First, accept what has happened and do your best to get along. You only hurt yourself if you resist. Second, hang in there. Remember you won't be there forever. There are lots of grown-up stepkids today, like me. We survived. And so can you.

In the early stages of living together, stepfamily members, like Gerri, begin to feel that life has played a terrible trick on them. They think the remarriage was a mistake and that all the members of the new household will never learn to get along. They say things like, "You're not my father," and "No child of mine would ever act like that," or "This is not a real family and I'm not a member." Disappointed and aggrieved, they may believe their lives have fallen to ruin and they'll never live happily again.

In working with stepfamilies, I've found that almost all of them experience disillusionment. In fact, stepfamilies go through a fairly predictable series of six adjustment stages that I call the stepfamily carousel. I call it that because learning to live in step is a little like riding a merry-go-round. You go up and down, round and round for a while, and it often seems you're not really getting anywhere. See if you can determine how many of the stages Gerri and her family passed through.

THE STEPFAMILY CAROUSEL

The getting acquainted stage. This is where the ride begins. The parents meet, begin to date and gradually begin to include their children in activities. Friendships are formed. Jealousy may begin to emerge.

The honeymoon stage. Excitement builds, the music quickens. Parents (and some kids) are delighted with the new relationships. The adults marry or begin living together. Friendships may deepen. But rivalry for attention, time, and love also become more pronounced.

The disillusionment stage. The ride becomes bumpy. Personal faults and flaws are exposed through the daily grind of going round and round together. Little irritations grow into major differences. Expectations are not met, so disappointment and disillusionment set in. Family members feel overwhelmed, resentful, helpless, or depressed. This stage may last for many long, exhausting months or even a few years.

The crisis point. The music falters, the carousel lurches, family members are in danger of falling off. Feelings that were repressed or hidden explode to the surface. Confrontations may occur between two, three, or all family members. Some members, fearful of confrontation, may withdraw or run away. A series of crisis points will likely occur alternately with other stages.

Reevaluation and decision. Each carousel rider looks back and decides whether to stay aboard. Consciously or unconsciously, family members determine whether to give up on making it as a family. If just one member is unwilling to try again, the family will remain unstable. An unbalanced carousel is wobbly.

Stages three, four and five will likely be repeated many times.

Equilibrium restored. The music becomes sweeter and the ride smoother. Family members have concluded that it is, indeed, worth staying together. There continue to be occasional disturbances; even the finest of carousels requires maintenance. But even in the midst of conflict, family members now have faith that, together, they can make it as a family. Their merry-go-round swings smoothly on.

Can you identify any stages your own family has experienced? What stage are you in now? If you're a member of two households, are there some similarities in the stages you have experienced in both? Some differences? It could be an interesting dinnertime conversation if you and your family discussed what stages you have passed through and what stages you may experience in the future.

There are many factors that affect how long each of the stages will last for you. One of those factors is the number of people in your stepfamily. The more people involved, the more complicated the process. Another element is the ages of the children. The younger a child is when remarriage occurs, the easier his or her adjustment will be. Also, when a parent has died (rather than divorced), the child is usually more reluctant to accept a stepparent.

There are many more cogs in the carousel wheel. For example, a stepparent who has never had children before generally has a harder time adjusting to stepfamily life than one who already is a parent. And because our society expects mothers to be especially close to their children and to do most of the disciplining, stepmothers and stepchildren usually have a harder time developing good relationships than stepfathers and stepchildren.

Another important factor in the ups and down of the carousel is the relationship of the child with the biological parent—the parent who lives in another home. If that parent is resentful or jealous of the stepparent, the young person will reflect that resentment. The greatest gift a divorced parent can give his or her child is permission to enjoy the other home, to like the other set of parents.

Other relatives influence the stepfamily's progress also. Grandparents, aunts, uncles, and others can help smooth the combination of two families into one. Or they can build boulder-sized roadblocks.

Tell your family about the stepfamily carousel. It often helps to know (especially when the ride is bumpy) that things won't always be the way they are today. Times change. People change. Relationships change. It also helps to know that disillusionment and crisis are normal. They're just stages in the natural cycle all stepfamilies pass through.

Like a carousel, life is often monotonous with its daily ups and downs. But stepfamilies that have passed through all six stages find that the ride, itself, can be worth the time. It can even be fun.

In the midst of crisis, however, this knowledge may not be enough to keep you going. I'd like to tell you about some resources hundreds of other stepfamilies have found useful.

STEPFAMILY ASSOCIATIONS

Many stepfamily members find their greatest source of help and comfort comes from others like themselves—other stepfamily members. Groups of stepfamilies are joining together in organizations all around the the country. They have programs, discussions, and parties. "We'd been everywhere for help," one stepparent said. "We were ready to give up. Then we started going to these regular stepfamily meetings. They're great!"

Stepchildren who talk with other stepchildren find they have much in common. And they often learn new ways to cope. The same is true for stepparents, grandparents, and others related to stepfamilies.

You and your family might enjoy getting together with other families like yourselves. Check the listing of places for help at the end of this book. Join a group that is near, or write for information about how to start a group.

COUNSELORS

People sometimes feel a little funny about going to a counselor. They see it as an admission of guilt or inadequacy. They fear exposing their private lives to an outsider. But going to a counselor is a positive step. It indicates courage and strength on the part of those who go. People who seek counseling are people who are willing to take charge of their lives, people who care.

What do counselors do? They listen; that may be the most important thing. They also guide families through the process of examining all sides of an issue. And they show respect for each person, each problem, each want and need.

A good counselor will act as an arbitrator bringing about negotiation, and as a teacher providing new ways to look at problems and respond to them. He or she will also point the way to other resources such as reading materials and support groups in the area. And a counselor will provide comfort.

When you and your family look for a counselor, check to see that he or she is familiar with stepfamily issues either through personal experience or special training. Professionals who have not had special training frequently are not well qualified to work with stepfamilies. A list of professionals in your area who have had at least some exposure to stepfamily issues may be obtained by writing to the Stepfamily Association of America, Inc., 900 Welch Road, Suite 400, Palo Alto, California 94304.

THE FAMILY CONFERENCE

A family conference is a gathering of all family members. Some families meet weekly at a regular time, others meet more or less often or at any time a member feels like having a meeting. Family conferences can be used to plan vacations, to work out household chore schedules, to share hobbies and other interests, to discuss problem issues (like discipline) and possible solutions, to plan fun activities, and for a hundred other purposes.

The family conference brings everyone together. It allows each to say what he or she is feeling and to know that those feelings are important. If used regularly, and for pleasant as well as not so pleasant tasks, it can help pull a stepfamily together.

CONTRACTS

A contract is a written and signed agreement which allows both or all parties involved to get (some of) what they want. For example, a teenager may want to be allowed to stay out later on weekends. A parent may want that teenager to get more rest. They both get what they want with a contract which says the teenager can stay out late on Saturday nights if he or she has been in bed by ten-thirty Monday through Thursday of that week.

Contracts can be used for almost any kind of issue. It often helps to have a third party help negotiate, write, and later reevaluate a contract. Soon, however, family members learn to negotiate and draw up their own.

How to Be Unhappy

Throughout the earlier chapters of this book, I have encouraged you to take care of yourself by speaking out, letting others know your feelings and desires, asking for your needs to be fulfilled. There are some things in life we can change—clothes, names, the way we communicate with others. And I have encouraged you to work hard at bringing about those changes which might make your life more satisfying.

But there are also a great many things in life we cannot change—the weather, our genetic heritage, whether a parent remarries and with whom. It is as important to know how to deal with these immutables as it is to know how to foster change. What things about your life might you be able to change? Which things are entirely beyond your control? How do you feel about the things you cannot change? What do you believe about them?

According to the famous psychologist Albert Ellis, it is not the events in our lives that make us happy or unhappy. Instead it is our beliefs about those events. First, an event occurs (like divorce or the remarriage of a parent). Second, we interpret or think of that event as terrible, horrible, etc. We may say things like, it's not fair, it shouldn't have happened, or why me? And then we are depressed as a result of our beliefs. Below is a list of beliefs that are guaranteed to make you unhappy.

1. My parents (stepparents, stepchildren) ought to be different than they are—nicer, neater, fairer, less strict, etc.

2. Those who have caused me pain should be punished.

3. I shouldn't have to put up with my stepbrother (stepsister, stepparent, stepchild).

4. I ought not lose my temper, make messes, yell at people, make mistakes.

5. I should be able to cope better, do things better, be a success.

6. Life shouldn't be so unfair.

Ellis explains that we can change our unhappiness by changing our beliefs. Examine your beliefs about life and about living in a stepfamily. Then take the advice of another great psychologist. "Don't should on yourself." You can get rid of a lot of unhappiness by getting rid of words like *should* and *ought*. When you find yourself thinking things *should* be different than they are, erase the thought. And watch out for other misery-making phrases like *it's horrible, it's unfair, it's bad,* etc. Replace them with the phrase, *it would be nice if;* it has a softer feel.

People who grow up with Eastern philosophies (Hindu, Buddhist, Tao, etc.) understand the flow of life in a different way than Westerners. They often see life as a river; it flows along and we with it. We can choose to resist and try to swim against the current, but we'll eventually be swept along anyway. Or we can choose to flow with the current, to relax and move with the stream of life.

Stepfamily members can think of themselves as troubled and disadvantaged; they can think of life as miserable and unfair. Or they can think of themselves as in the midst of a challenging journey, as having an opportunity to learn, grow, and change.

Have you ever seen the place where two creeks or streams come together? There's noisy turbulence where they join. It's as if the waters of the two are fighting. But downstream they flow smoothly; the two have become one river.

The joining of two families causes noisy turbulence, too. The two families often struggle and fight with one another.

But soon, downstream, things even out. If the stepfamily members work hard at changing the things they can and accepting those they cannot change, soon they'll flow smoothly along together; they'll be one family.

Places For Help

Kids' Stuff

National Runaway
Switchboard
800-621-4000

Call this number free from any location in the United States if you need help or want to contact relatives.

National Runaway Hotline
800-392-3352

Call if you wish to leave a message for friends or relatives or for help of any kind.

Child Abuse Hotline
800-252-5400

Call free for information about what to do if you are being abused.

Operation Venus
800-227-8922

Call free for information and help concerning VD (venereal disease).

International Youth
Council (IYC)
7910 Woodmont Avenue
Washington, DC 20814

A division of Parents Without Partners. Offers help for teens who have a single parent. Chapters in over 100 cities.

Alateen
Alanon Family Group Help
1 Park Avenue
New York, NY 10016

A branch of Alcoholics Anonymous for teens with parents who drink too much. Look under Alcoholics Anonymous in your phone directory or write this address.

Planned Parenthood
810 Seventh Avenue
New York, NY 10010

Provides birth-control information and counseling. Look in your phone directory or write this address.

If you need a place to go to get your troubles off your mind or just for fun and friendship, check your phone directory for Boys Clubs, Girls Clubs, YWCA, YMCA, or community centers. Look in the Yellow Pages under Youth Organizations and Centers.

Stepfamily Organizations

The Stepfamily Association of America, Inc.
900 Welch Road, Suite 400
Palo Alto, CA 94304

Local chapters in most cities. Offers educational material, stepfamily survival courses, referral services, newsletter. Write for address of chapter nearest you.

Remarrieds, Inc.
Box 742
Santa Ana, CA 92701

Offers educational and social programs. Several local chapters.

Step Family Foundation, Inc.
333 West End Avenue
New York, NY 10023

Offers individual and family counseling in New York and selected areas. Newsletter.

Remarried Parents, Inc.
c/o Temple Beth Sholom
172 Second Street and
Northern Boulevard
Flushing, NY 11358

Monthly meetings, lectures, weekly support groups, socials. Provides children's services.

Stepparent Education Workshops
Community Mental-Health Center
Cedars-Sinai Medical Center
Los Angeles, CA 90048

Sponsored by Thalians. Offers educational workshops for stepparents in the Los Angeles area. Write for more information.

Remarried Association of
Long Island
852 Prescott Street
Valley Stream, NY 11580

Regular meetings, counseling,
social events. Speakers bureau.

The Sand Dollar Family
Works
716 Chelsea Place
Houston, TX 77006

Offers group seminars for
children and parents of
separated, divorced and
remarried families.

Parents' Groups

Parents Anonymous
2810 Artesia Boulevard,
Suite F
Redondo Beach, CA 90278

Help for parents of abused
children. Write for free
information.

Batterers Anonymous
P.O. Box 29
Redlands, CA 92373

Weekly meetings for men. Write
for free information.

Divorce Anonymous
P.O. Box 5313
Chicago, IL 60680

Regular meetings for the
divorced. Write for nearest local
group.

Parents Without Partners
7910 Woodmont Ave, Suite
1000
Washington, DC 20014

Meetings for single parents.
Check phone book for local
group or write this address.

Single Dads' Hotline
P.O. Box 4842
Scottsdale, AZ 85258
602-998-0980

Assists divorced fathers living all
over United States. Call for
information.

National Self-Help
Clearinghouse
City University Graduate
Center
33 West Forty-second
Street
New York, NY 10036

Write for information about
other self-help groups in your
area, or for information about
how to start a group.

For counseling help, check your local phone book for Family Counseling Services. For a list of counselors in your area who have special
training in stepfamily issues, write the Stepfamily Association of
America, 900 Welch Road, Suite 400, Palo Alto, California 94304.

About The Author

Linda Craven is on the editorial staff of the *Stepfamily Bulletin*, a national journal for which she also writes a children's column. A member of the board of directors of the Stepfamily Association of America, Inc., she assists in the organization of local chapters. She and her family are members of the Panhandle Stepfamily Association, a group which they helped found. Ms. Craven's work appears in a wide variety of magazines and newspapers. She leads workshops for stepfamilies, teachers and counselors, writers, young people, and church groups.

A native Texan, she attended Texas Tech, Texas A & I, and West Texas State Universities. After receiving B.A. and M.A. degrees, she worked as a teacher, a counselor, and as a church-school director. She continues to serve as a religious education and growth consultant to churches and fellowships.

Linda is a stepmother. She and her husband Jerry, who is a professor of English literature and a writer, have a total of four children. They live in Texas.